Running From The Wolf

A Big Woods Pack Novel: Book Two

Written by:

Cara Roman

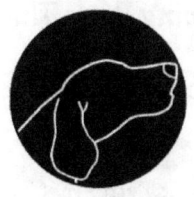

Baying Hound's Dark Side

USA

Disclaimers and Copyright

This is a work of fiction. Names, characters, places, and incidents either are a product of the author's imagination or are used fictitiously. Any resemblance to actual persons, living or dead, events or locations is entirely coincidental.

Running From The Wolf

A Big Woods Pack Novel: Book Two

Published by Baying Hound's Dark Side

ISBN: 978-0-9988282-8-2

Chapter 1

Trying to ignore all of the hushed gossip around her, Kayla was struggling to get through her shift. It had been insanely busy at Dusty's Roadhouse ever since the house fire at Gerald and Cathy Wyles' house that killed so many people. It was big news in this sleepy little Michigan town where nothing much ever really happens. Normally most people spent winter evenings tucked into their warm homes, and this was the slow season at work, with it picking up as the weather warmed. Death will do that though, bring everyone out to reminisce, and hear all the juicy details. Of course nobody here knew the real story of what had happened to those people, and listening to how great so and so was, or how sorry everyone was about not getting over to visit them more often was starting to get to Kayla. Every single one of those people had a choice in their fate, and the consequences of that choice was their death. Maybe if they had believed her brother Kian, there wouldn't have been a battle among the pack. Then she wouldn't have had to drag their bodies from Kian's yard, load them into their own cars, and place them throughout the Wyles' home. There wouldn't have been a fire at all.

The more people droned on about the tragedy the more it just made Kayla angry. Remembering the way Cathy Wyles and her husband Gerald had attempted to kill her brother's mate Emma it was all Kayla could do to stop the growl from rumbling in her throat. She wasn't sorry that she and Emma had killed the older couple. In her world, you either stopped the threat coming for you, or you died. Kayla had stopped it, but damn it, she would like to have clued everyone in here in to exactly how cruel and selfish those 'victims' had been on their final day. They died with snarls in their throat, and blood on their teeth trying to tear Emma apart.

Shaking her head to rid herself of that image, Kayla hustled from table to table. Refilling drinks, and taking orders. Everyone expected witty banter with an easy smile from her, so she did her best to make sure that is exactly what they got. Counting down the hours until her shift ended, Kayla decided tonight she was going to shift and roam the woods. Kayla might have been on the smaller side for a woman, but her wolf was fierce. Dominant, and always ready for action. Mom used to say that she was going the be a hell raiser when she was little. But that was before Dad died. Kayla just couldn't put her mother through more heart ache after that. So she was always in a battle of wills with the wolf inside of her. Most of the time she was able to calm her wolf down. That was difficult lately. Too much had been happening, and her wolf was on edge.

At least Emma was able to go back to her nursing job at the clinic. That freed up a lot of time for Kayla, since she had been taking turns guarding her. Now that Kayla had turned Emma, she had the tools to defend herself from danger. They were all being careful though, because her bastard of an uncle was still hiding out there somewhere. Kayla hoped he came sneaking back into Big Woods pack territory, he had a lot to pay for. Vengeance should go to Emma for the murder of her parents, and Kian as the new Alpha, but Kayla wouldn't mind watching it all unfold. While Kayla was envisioning dear, sweet, evil uncle Russ with his throat ripped out Kole and Jase walked in. Settling in at the bar Kole gave her a nod, and Jase smiled. He surprised her when he tossed his fate in with theirs recognizing Kian as his new Alpha. But had he not taken their side things might have worked out differently. The odds still hadn't been in their favor, but that extra fighter definitely helped.

"It's busy as all hell in here today boys, hope you got lots of patience if you're wanting food," Kayla said as she grabbed them each a beer.

"Sure is. Everyone wants to see what everyone else knows. No one has any different information though. At least you're getting good tips out of the chaos I guess," Kole said taking a sip of his beer. "I've got plenty of time," looking over at Jase, who nodded in agreement, "How about some burgers, fries, and a large hot wings to share. Thanks Kay."

"You better be leaving me some good tips too." She narrowed her eyes at them before heading back into the kitchen to put their order in and grab another tray of food. Thankfully, the new girl Wendy was better at her job than her predecessor had been. She was practically running to keep up, but she was getting the right food to each table, and keeping the drinks filled. Which was all anyone could ask of her. That she was a looker, although very married, definitely helped smooth over any mistakes she made along the way. The guys were devouring wings, fingers covered in hot sauce when she checked on them next. Carl the lazy bartender must have gotten their appetizer to them. That meant he was going to want to split the damn tip. Shaking her head she asked them how things were.

"I wanted to talk to you about helping out in the office now that, well you know. Jase and I are pretty swamped at the job site, and we could use Kian there at least some of the week." Kole gave her his most charming smile. And boy, was it a doozy of a smile too. Women all over West Michigan fell into bed with him because of that. His dark hair, the steel blue Decker eyes, and shifter muscles certainly didn't hurt either. As his sister though Kayla was immune to his charm, and well versed in his tricks.

"I don't know, Kole. I live with you, I don't want to work with you and Kian too. I already want to strangle you on a semi-regular basis." Kian didn't harass her the way Kole always had, but he was forever going to see her as his baby sister with pig tails in her hair. Which wasn't much better in her opinion.

"Come on Kayla, okay, look, in all seriousness it would be a shame if we fell behind on our deadlines, and tanked the family business. At least until we can hire some more people."

"Including a new secretary?" She tilted her head suspiciously.

"Yeah, absolutely." Kole nodded at her, his dark hair flopping forward into his eyes.

"Fine, but you owe me. You're on cleanup at home for a month." Kayla smiled deviously as she walked away. Getting out of cleaning the house for the next while definitely helped alleviate some of her annoyance. The added money she would be making wouldn't hurt either.

The crowd dissipated after dinner, leaving only a few tables still occupied. Carl announced that he needed a break, heading out back to smoke. Ha! Like he was the one running around this place all night. Kayla manned the bar, while Wendy easily handled the floor. She was straightening the bottles of liquor on the mirrored shelves hanging up on the wall behind the bar when Deputy Lex Kolter walked in. She caught his scent even before she heard some diners calling out in greeting. Inhaling deeply, he always smelled like pine trees and sunshine to Kayla. It made her knees go weak, and put her back up in equal measure. Reminding herself there was no use wanting someone that was completely uninterested in you after all. Who cares that he wore that uniform like it was painted on, every muscle on display? Or that his warm brown eyes looked like melted chocolate, and his brown hair shone streaks of gold.

It was definitely best to ignore the sexy new scruffy stubble he was sporting lately.

Taking a deep breath to calm her hormones as he sat down next to Jase at the bar. Arranging her face in carefully neutral lines Kayla walked over with his drink. Cherry coke in a Styrofoam to go cup since he was on duty. "Eating dinner tonight Deputy?"

He looked at her for a minute, before saying. "No, just the pop, thanks." Sounding completely worn out. He always did that, stared at her like she was dangerous to him, and he needed to be at the ready to take evasive action.

"Anything new?" Kole asked quietly. They all knew what he was asking without having to go into more detail than that.

"Naw, we're good. Just got done on patrol for the night, about to head into the station and finish up some paperwork. Thought I would grab a drink to take back with me. See how things were going."

"Our girl here was running around all night it was so damn busy in this place," Jase said tipping the neck of his beer bottle in her direction. He didn't notice the way Lex's eyes narrowed marginally. "You know how people get. Out gossiping, wanting to see what everyone else has heard about what's goin' on."

"That I do. I've been bombarded with questions everywhere I go lately," he said taking a pull on his straw, tasting his drink. "Mmm, extra cherries, thanks Kayla. Well, that paperwork isn't going to write itself. Guess I better head on out." He stood up to go, but paused a moment. "We still on for Kian's house this weekend?"

"Yeah, he said every Sunday, and Emma mentioned a pot roast. See you there, man," Kole said as Lex gave him a goodbye slap on the back, and nodded his head before walking out the door.

"Always wondered why you don't like Lex, Kayla," Jase asked watching her closely and absentmindedly peeling the blue label from his bottle.

"He just gets on my nerves is all. Always has," she answered back wiping down the top of the big wooden bar, darkened with age. It wasn't completely a lie, he did get on her nerves, but she had a lifetime of practice hiding the rest of what she felt. Jase raised an eyebrow at her, but didn't comment any further. Kayla took that as her cue to find busy work avoiding more questions until they left for the night.

Carl came back from his break just in time to help her cash everyone out. Weeknights they closed up at eleven pm. She was cleaning the place with Wendy when she asked her if she was seeing anyone. Laughingly Kayla shook her head. "Nope, why, you wanna take me out on a date? What would your husband think?"

"I doubt Brad would mind me putting the moves on you. Hell Kayla, he would probably be game to watch. But sadly you're just not my type. Actually, I was thinking you might want to see a movie with us, kind of a double date, with his friend from work, Sam." Looking over at Kayla she added, "But If you're not interested it could just be a friend type thing."

Thinking it had been way too long since she went on a date of any kind, even a blind date, possibly friend type double date. She could use a distraction, and if it was a bust, then she didn't have to go out with him again, or give him her number. "Yeah, okay, when were you thinking?"

"Well, its short notice, but this place is closed tomorrow, would that work? I don't know what's playing yet, but I can look up sometimes and text you?" Wendy said grinning from ear to ear.

"Okay, text me the details. I don't really have a preference, whatever you wanna see works. I do have some things to take care of early on, so evening definitely works better for me," Kayla smiled, stacking chairs on tables as Wendy mopped. Today had sure started shitty, but it was ending on a much better note.

Usually she cranked the music up when she was driving, but tonight she just wasn't in the mood to let the music soothe her. She was tired of pretending things were alright, spent all day at work faking it. Tonight she allowed the anger, and frustration build inside of her. Anger at all that happened, anger at her uncle's betrayal, and anger at having to pretend she wasn't angry in the first place.

Noticing Kole had most of the lights out in the house they shared, the one they had grown up in, she pulled her SUV into the garage. The one in his room was on, and the light over the stove had been left on. Probably for her. As shifters they could see well in the dark, but it was still a welcoming sight when someone cared enough to leave a light on for you. Walking inside she tossed her coat over the back of the teal sofa, and set her purse down on the kitchen counter. Her work clothes went into the hamper in the laundry room. Striding through the house completely naked she walked through the back door. Closing it softly behind her she took one deep breath to brace herself for the inevitable pain of the shift, and let her wolf have her.

After so many years of practice the change happened swiftly. Had anyone been watching it would have looked like the cream-colored wolf had simply burst from Kayla's skin. Of course, it happened muscle by muscle, with each bone reshaping to her new form. Shaking off the residual energy Kayla leaped off the back porch and raced across the yard into the tree line. Her paws sinking into the snow with each step, she weaved around trees jumping the occasional log. The musky smell of deer hit her nostrils and she considered it a moment; the chase would be fun. But it would just have been a waste since she wasn't hungry right then. Instead she ran past everyone's homes. As she passed Kian's place she picked up the sound of their lovemaking with her sensitive ears. Not wanting to intrude on their privacy she pushed herself faster. Jase's house was next, just a cabin in the woods really, all the lights were off, and judging by the soft steady sound of his breathing he was fast asleep.

Looping back around and slowing her pace she rounded the bend at Lex's. He had a small house, neighboring her own home. They grew up a yard away from each other. But it might as well have been an ocean apart considering the distance between them. The light in his office was on, he was probably hunting down leads on her uncle's whereabouts. He didn't sleep enough lately. The stress was making him push himself too hard in her opinion.

Reminding herself that wasn't her business, denying herself the lonesome howl her throat yearned for, she ran off. Towards the acrid smell of smoke. There wasn't much left to the Wyles' house anymore, completely destroyed inside, with large sections of the roof having blown off in the explosion. One back corner still stood, but what the fire hadn't eaten away at the spray the firemen doused it with had taken care of. A satisfying growl rumbled low in her throat. She was happy nothing of the house was salvageable. Her pack would heal better once it was razed to the ground completely.

Satisfied all was well with her pack tonight, and having drained the anger out of her system Kayla turned towards home. Once on the back porch she stretched as a wolf and tucked her away again until next time. Fur receded, paws turned back into hands and feet, her muzzle shortened into a mouth and nose. Tipping her head toward her shoulder, one side then the other she worked the kinks out before opening the door and heading on up to bed. She would be able to sleep better now.

Chapter 2

Walking into Decker Construction bright and early the next morning taking a sip from the steaming paper cup of mocha from the shop in town Kayla sighed. It had been so long since she stepped foot in this place. Back when her Dad was alive she had been in and out of here. But after he died there hadn't been much reason for it. She wasn't going to be joining the crew swinging a hammer, and it had felt empty without her father's voice filling the space. The layout was exactly as she remembered it, though the decor had been updated at some point in the last ten years. The small reception area immediately to the right consisted of two chairs and a wooden end table between them stacked with home magazines. There were stunning 'after' pictures showcasing their work in large frames on the wall. Nestled in the corner was a small beverage area, a pod style coffee machine, and a spinning carousel of different flavored brews and teas to choose from. A small basket held sugar packets, and little cups of creamer like the gas station had. The left held a decent sized desk, completely empty of everything except a computer monitor, keyboard and telephone. With a wall of shelves behind filled with binders housing paperwork, and some design books. Next to the desk was a locked filing cabinet. Directly in front of the door across the room was a hallway that had a small bathroom halfway down, and the open door at the end was her brother Kian's new office.

Kayla headed on back to talk to her brother. Seated behind his desk Kian was running his hands exasperatedly through his hair when she stepped into the office. "Hey Kay, ah, I'm just trying to figure out how I'm going to get everything done on time. What brings you in? Please tell me nothing broke at the house, or you didn't get a wild hair up your ass and want to redo it?" His eyes shining with something close to panic as he said the last part.

"No, ya big dummy. I'm here to save your bacon, by volunteering my help with whatever office work you might need. I used to work summers and weekends here as a teenager, before, well you know. So I'm sure I can be of use to you. I have plans later this evening, but other than that my day is yours. Tomorrow I will change my availability to evenings only at Dusty's until you can hire someone else here. That should free you up some to go help out the guys on site." Kayla beamed at him, "You can thank me now."

Standing up and rounding the desk so fast he practically blurred Kian wrapped her up in a big ol' bear hug and spun her around. "You are my favorite sister Kay!"

Laughing at her big brother's relief she said, "Yeah well I'm your only sister, but I'll take it. But don't you think for one second you don't have to pay me. I might be willing to help, but I still have bills to pay."

Kian stopped spinning and set her back down. "I can pay you exactly as much as Cathy was making, which by the way came with full benefits, and paid vacation time in case you decide on staying."

"How much is that?" Kayla asked hoping that it was enough to justify her time. She made decent tips during the lunch rush at work.

"Fifteen dollars an hour," he said walking back behind his desk. "It's all we can afford right now."

Holy crap. That was more than she was expecting. She would be able to pay her car off much faster making that kind of money. "That works for me Kian, bring me up to speed."

He grabbed some files off his desk handed them over to her. "We are working on these two jobs right now. One is a whole house renovation, the other one a master bathroom only. That one should be done in the next day or so. Once that one is finished we have a few weeks to devote completely to the first job. Then as soon as the snow melts and the ground thaws we have a house slated to build. That one we will be hiring out some subcontractors to help with. I was in the process of getting with some people about that and nailing down prices and timelines when you walked in. Cathy kept the schedule, handled estimates, and as you remember greeted walk ins, answered the phone."

"Not a problem. I noticed her desk was cleared out, has her computer been wiped too?" Kayla asked as she walked around his office looking at the pictures on the wall. There was one of the whole family at Kian's graduation, before Dad passed away. Another of Kian standing next to Lex and Kole as teenagers on the beach at Lake Michigan. And one of Emma, out in the back yard of his house, she was looking past the camera at the photographer with a smile that lit her whole face up. The wind was lifting her auburn hair up, and there was a fresh blanket of snow on the ground. "That is an amazing shot of Emma. What did you say to make her smile like that?"

Looking all business, "Not completely. Everything pertaining to the company was left on it." Then Kian's face softened, "I asked her if she wanted to make snow angels. She lit right up and told me it was something she had always wanted to do." One corner of his mouth tipped up in a dreamy smile remembering that moment with his mate. "She is amazing."

"I know Kian, I love her too," Kayla said. "I'm going to set myself up out there. Let me know if you need anything." She hung her coat up in the small closet and walked back out front. Booting the computer up she read through everything, familiarizing herself. The phone rang about an hour later, and just like old times she said, "Good morning, Decker Construction, how may I assist you today?"

It was the couple having the house built this spring calling to let them know they were newly pregnant, and wanted to know if they could come in and adjust the plans making room for a nursery. Smiling at the sound of their joy she told them congratulations, and Mr. Decker was free this afternoon. They agreed on a time, and Kayla typed it into Kian's schedule. Hanging up Kayla was still smiling when Deputy Kolter walked in.

"Hey, Deck!" Lex said angling his head back towards Kian's office, then looking over at her,

"Good afternoon Kayla, you look really happy today." Before she could respond Kian walked up saying it was probably because she had a date tonight.

"Excuse me, how exactly do you know I have a date tonight, brother?" She caught him with a dirty look.

"You said you had plans tonight. You're wearing a dress, and you have perfume on. Add it up, and it equals a date," Kian shrugged.

"Who are you going out with?" Lex stared down at where she was seated behind the desk. His tone was decidedly less friendly than it had been a minute ago. His moods always gave her whiplash.

"That is none of your damn business Deputy Kolter." She crossed her arms. "And this isn't exactly fancy, I'm not even showing any skin," Kayla pointed out. She had on a sapphire blue turtleneck sweater dress, charcoal gray tights, with small silver hoops hanging from her ears, and black knee-high low-heeled boots.

"How much skin do you usually show on dates?" Lex was openly glaring at her now. Kian was looked at her like he wasn't sure he wanted to know the answer. Well good, he should be uncomfortable.

Raising an eyebrow at both of the idiotic men, "That depends on whether I plan on getting laid or not." Kian burst out laughing, and there was silver starting to swirl in Lex's warm chocolate eyes. "Since I am going on a blind double date with the new waitress Wendy and her husband Brad, to the movies I might add, no skin was the best option tonight."

"Well good Kayla, you haven't gone on a date in a while," Kian said. "It may just be that I'm newly mated and all, but I'm happy for you."

"Thanks for your approval, but since I'm not out to find a mate it's not needed. And next time you want to keep track of how long my dry spell has been, don't." Kayla sat back down.

"I'm sorry, I didn't mean it like that, shit." Kian shook his head and gestured for Lex to walk back to the office with him.

Lex was here in an official capacity, to collect the box of belongings that had been cleared off

Cathy's old desk. The two of them talked about how the hunt for Russell was going, apparently not very well, the old bastard was really good at covering his tracks. Kian asked Lex if he had told his folks about Emma being his Dad's sister's daughter. He hadn't yet, what with all the hours he was putting in with the fire. It had been ruled accidental, but that didn't mean there wasn't a bunch of paperwork, and Lex stayed on top of everything making sure nothing suspicious came up that could point back to them. That was the perk of a pack member being on with the police. He was in place and available to sweep any mention of the pack under the rug. That's the way shifters operated, they policed themselves. Jail time just wasn't an option when someone could shift into an animal, exposing all of them.

Kayla got a text message from Wendy letting her know they were going to the seven fifteen showing of the new action movie. Lots of sweaty muscled men, cool stunts, car chases, guns, and the obligatory explosion. Kayla wasn't really surprised; it was a safe choice as far as movies went. Too romantic and it would seem like they were pushing her towards Sam too much, same goes for a scary movie. The choice was down to an action movie, or a comedy movie. Kayla was letting Wendy know that sounded great to her, and that she would meet them there when Lex walked back out.

"Have fun on your date tonight," he growled out as he walked past her.

The nerve of that guy. Standing up and storming out she caught him as he was opening the driver's side door to his white and gold county sheriff's cruiser. "What exactly is your problem?" she said looking up at him. At five foot three she looked up at most people.

"Not a damn thing. Don't let me keep you from going out with some fucker you don't even know. But hey, I'm sure he's a great catch, aside from the fact that he has to have his friends get his dates for him. I'm sure you will have a great time with his arm around your shoulder." No mistaking the silver swirling in his eyes now. The smell of fur coming off his skin was drowning out the pine and sunshine of his normal scent.

"Are you serious right now?" she said on a growl. "You had your chance with me Alexander Kolter! You didn't want me, and if memory serves, you said that I wasn't enough of a woman for you. So you can take your opinions on my love life, and shove them right up your ass! And furthermore, if I don't want someone's arm on my shoulder, or any other part of them touching me you best believe I am more than capable of handing them their balls." How dare he judge her? What kind of ass hat did that! Not waiting for his response, she turned and walked away.

"OK, what the hell is going on here?" Kian asked her as soon as she was back inside the office.

"You're about a decade late to this party Kian. I don't want to talk about it. It's over and done with." Kayla sat down in her chair.

"A decade ago you were sixteen. What happened between you and my then twenty-year-old best friend?" Kian added a little Alpha push to the question making it impossible for her not to answer him.

"Ugh, that is not very cool, Kian. Fine. He stopped by the house one night, you and Kole were both working late finishing up some job. Mom and Dad were out on a date. I was about to make a sandwich for myself, and told Lex to come on in, I would make him one too. No big, he was always around. We sat there eating and talking for a while. Then when we were cleaning up the kitchen he kissed me. Just leaned down and pressed his lips to mine, like he had done it a thousand times before. When he pulled away I kept my eyes closed for a moment smiling to myself, swimming in happiness. When I opened them he was gone. I asked him the next time I saw him what happened, and he told me that he made a mistake, and he was a grown man and shouldn't have taken advantage of me like that. I told him I wasn't a little kid, and that I liked him kissing me. He said that I might as well have been," Kayla said dejectedly.

"Holy mother fucking shit! Lex kissed you? You and Lex?" Kian looked like he was about to implode.

"You know, for a powerful dominant man who can sense a lie, you are an idiot," Kayla told him. "I have always had a thing for Lex. Ever since I can remember. Hell, what girl doesn't have the hots for her older brother's friends? When he kissed me I thought that the planets had aligned or something. But he couldn't see me as anything past your baby sister I guess."

"True, he knew I would have kicked his ass if I had known." Kian nodded his head. "But I am sorry it hurt you Kay."

"Dad knew. I was pacing my room after talking to Lex. Torn between anger and pain. I was trying to decide if I should go over there and kick his ass, or kiss him with everything I had to prove I wasn't some little girl anymore. He sat me down and explained that Lex was probably just scared by how big I was in his life. That it was a hard thing to have feelings for your best friend's sister. He was trying to respect you, not break me. He said, 'give it time, little one hmm, that boy will come around.' But he never did, Kian. So he has no say in what I do, or whom."

Chapter 3

The rest of the day went by quickly since she was working off a decent mad. Kayla considered canceling on the date, but that was too close to letting Lex win. So after going home to grab a quick bite to eat she was heading the next town over to the theater. It wasn't one of those big multiplexes with a dozen different screens and fancy seating. There were three screens, with traditional rows of movie seats. Wendy and her husband Brad were waiting in the lobby for her when she walked in. Wendy wore dark skinny jeans tucked into camel-colored boots, and under her coat was a white V-neck sweater, which showcased her olive skin and dark hair to perfection. Kayla gave her a hug before turning to smile at her husband Brad. He was light to her dark with reddish blonde hair, and fair skin. He had an easy smile, and they fit really well together.

Just as she was about to ask where their friend was he walked over. "Hey, you must be Kayla, I'm Sam. The loser who needs his friends to set him up apparently." He was laughing as he held his hand out to her.

Liking that he could joke about this and put her more at ease she shook his hand. No spark zinged between their hands, but then Kayla hadn't expected one. "Well, I guess with those parameters, I'm a loser too. I agreed to a blind date too."

"Well, since we are both hopeless let's go watch a movie that has nothing at all to do with love." He held his arm out gesturing her to walk in front of him.

They picked seats somewhere in the middle with Sam, Kayla, Wendy, and then Brad being the sitting order. It reminded her a little of high school, especially if Wendy and Brad decided to make out during the movie. Since the house lights were dimming as they sat down there was no time for conversation. She looked over at Sam. He was a good looking guy, and seemed nice. Wishing she was more attracted to him she sighed. His hair was the wrong shade of brown, more bark than golden. His eyes were edging towards hazel instead of a dark melting brown. It was always like this. She always found herself steering away from brunettes because they made her want Lex more. She could admit it to herself, hell her wolf had been screaming it at her for the last decade. But Kayla couldn't force the man to want her, and she wasn't the kind of woman who begged for a man's attention. She still had her pride.

About halfway through the movie Sam stretched his arm across the back of her chair, and it just didn't feel right. He was nice, and it wasn't like he was groping her, or anything. But it was Lex's stupid remark about her having his arm around her shoulder. Wishing she could forget what he said, but knowing it wasn't possible, she crossed her legs angling her body away from Sam towards Wendy. He got the hint and removed his arm. He stayed to his side of the armrest after that. The movie was exactly as Kayla expected, and it didn't disappoint. Thinking it would be a good one to watch at home with Kole when it came out she followed the throng of people out the doors. Back out in the lobby she headed for the bathroom, and Wendy tagged along.

"So, what do you think of Sam?" Wendy asked staring at her in the mirror while she slicked on some lip stick.

Kayla finished washing her hands before replying. "He seems like a really nice guy. I just don't think that we clicked. I'm sorry. Thanks for inviting me out though."

"Yeah, I didn't think it was going anywhere. But I thought I would ask. Want to get some food, or are you just heading home?" she asked as they walked out of the bathroom and met up with the guys.

"I had a good time, the movie was cool. But I ate beforehand. Plus, I have a early morning tomorrow if I'm going to fit both jobs in," Kayla shrugged.

"I didn't know you had another job."

"I just started today. I'm doing office work at my family's construction company. I have to change my hours of availability at Dusty's." They walked outside standing in front of the theater. "It was nice to meet you Brad, Wendy talks about you all the time." Turning towards Sam with an apologetic shrug she added, "it was nice meeting you too." He nodded his head with a slight smile, message received, there would be no other dates.

"I guess that means more hours for me. I could use them too. See you at work then," Wendy said lacing her fingers through her husband's and heading towards their car.

Waving at them Kayla walked to her burgundy SUV. The drive home was pretty uneventful, she kept the music low singing along quietly. Pulling into her drive she remembered to turn her phone back on. There was a text from Emma telling her to have fun on her date with a winky face. Clearly Kian had filled his mate in on her plans for the evening. As she was about to put it back in her purse it rang. The display telling her it was Lex. Thinking to herself shit, why was he calling? She put the phone to her ear.

"Deputy Kolter." Hating that her voice sounded clipped and angry as it usually did with him. She couldn't seem to help it.

"Hey, Kay." She winced at the nickname everyone used. He hadn't called her that in a long time. "I wanted to apologize for getting angry today. It wasn't fair to you." He sounded torn up.

"No, it wasn't fair, but I understand. I always get really mad at you too. Guess maybe we shouldn't be around each other," she said, thinking that wouldn't be very easy.

"We both know that's not possible, especially in such a small pack. Actually, I wanted to know if you could come over for a minute. I know its late, but I wanted to talk to you."

"It's only nine thirty." Softening just a little she added, "I just pulled in at home, so give me a minute and I will be there, okay?" He had never asked her to come over to his place. Sure she had been over at his parents numerous times growing up, but when Lex bought his own place she wasn't exactly close with him anymore.

Pulling the visor down and looking in the mirror at herself Kayla gave her short hair a tousle. Taking a deep breath, she put the visor back, started the car again, and backed out of the drive. She had an understanding with Kole. They weren't each other's keeper, and as adults could come and go as they pleased, no questions asked. So she knew he wouldn't worry over her getting home just to leave again. The drive over to Lex's place was a short one. He may not live next door anymore, but he was only a few acres away. He had a small house, and she had stared endlessly at it as a wolf so she knew the basic layout. He didn't really use the front door, so once she parked in the drive she walked up to the side door next to the garage.

Before she could bang her knuckles against the wood he had it open. Lex in a uniform was a sight to see, and he probably gave all the women in town cop fantasies. But when he was dressed down in regular clothes, he reminded her of the Lex she used to know, and all those years of pining for him growing up. It was that much harder on her heart seeing him in the jeans and faded red t-shirt. His gold-streaked brown hair was messily standing on end, and he was barefoot. Doing her best to shore up her defenses she gave him a quirky head tilt as she walked in.

"Thanks for coming over. Do you want a drink? I was having a beer," he said, looking at the ground and running his hand over his head. Kayla surmised that was how his hair got to be so disheveled. He used to do that all the time, but while he was in uniform he shut down those mindless habits.

"Uh, sure. A beer would be okay." She followed him towards the kitchen. It was a small galley style, but with gleaming white counter tops and black cabinets. It looked timeless and classic. He pulled a bottle of beer out of the refrigerator twisting the metal cap off before handing it to her. Kayla gave herself points for not pointing out that she could have opened it herself. But since he was making an effort to be nice she would try too.

Lex gestured for her to head into the living room. Also on the small side it had moss green walls, and a tan couch with a scuffed up coffee table in front of it. His beer was already sitting on it, without a coaster Kayla noted, and there was a hockey game muted on the big screen TV that hung from the wall. Lex had always loved the Red Wings. "I hope I didn't ruin your date with what I said earlier. It was an asshole move, you were right to call me out on it. I just, it's just, well I mean, I don't know," he muttered shaking his head. Clearly he wasn't sure what he wanted to say.

"Don't worry about it. I went because I hadn't gone out much lately, it's not like I was looking for a mate. The movie was good, but he never had a chance." Sipping her beer she continued, "He's a brunette."

"A brunette? Really, what's wrong with that?" Lex looked over at her confused.

"I have a strict no brunette rule when it comes to men." Kayla shrugged. "I just can't date 'em." She took another drink of her beer, crossing one leg up over the other. The couch wasn't half bad. Sure it lacked a spunky color, but it made up for it with basic comfort.

"Can't? You have gorgeous brown hair Kayla, I don't get why you wouldn't like men who have brown hair." Lex seemed genuinely baffled.

"Because of you." At his intake of breath, and quick look at her Kayla knew that got to him. "None of them are right. I don't have as much of a problem if I avoid brunettes all together."

"I turned you off guys with brown hair completely? Wow, that's some talent." He looked away finishing the last of his beer.

Rushing to explain, she said, "I'm sorry, I really shouldn't have said anything. I didn't mean it as a slap this time. It's not that you turned me off them, it's that none of them are you. I can forget it's really you I want kissing me when the guy has blonde hair, but I can't separate you from that moment when he doesn't. Sam, the guy tonight, he had brown hair with brown eyes. I knew as soon as I saw him it wasn't going anywhere." Kayla was definitely rambling now. She had a tendency to do that when she was nervous. Being near Lex usually made her either nervous or angry.

"Wait. Back up, you're thinking of me when another man is kissing you?" He leaned forward resting his arms on his knees, holding his head. "What am I supposed to do with that Kay? I have spent every day of the last ten years holding myself back from you."

"Well, you didn't have to. I spent a long time waiting for you to stop doing that," Kayla said. "I should go. It's easier when your Deputy Kolter instead of just Lex."

Before she could get up he turned towards her, reaching out his hand cupping her cheek. "I'm still Lex with the uniform on too."

Undone by his touch after all this time, she nuzzled her face into his hand, and he sighed. Locking eyes with her he leaned towards her slowly. His lips touched hers in a soft kiss, and then everything pent up for the last decade came rushing forward like the dam bursting. She licked the seam of his mouth demanding, not asking for entry. As soon as her tongue found his Lex let out a groan and pulled her up against him. Kayla was lost in the taste of him. Her wolf howling inside for more. Taking handfuls of his hair she pressed her breasts against him. Her body was on fire, and she could smell the pheromones pouring off him too.

Lex reached down and pulled her sweater dress over her head in one swoop. Looking down at the gauzy sheer blue bra she was wearing he said reverently, "Dear god, you matched," as his big hands palmed her. She was a slim woman, with a compact body. His big hands covered the entirety of her breasts, gripping them. The sensation of the sheer material pressing and rubbing against her nipples felt so good, so right. Needing to see more of him she was tugging at his shirt when he reached back with one hand and pulled it over his head.

Kayla ran her hands down his muscles like she had always longed to do. Digging her nails in just enough that he felt the bite. She was working the button of his jeans desperate to free his dick while he pushed and pulled her tights down, taking the panties along with. As soon as his dick popped free of his pants she was on it. Gliding her tongue up from the base tasting the saltiness of his skin. When her lips wrapped around the head and sucked him into her mouth he groaned and reached down to find her clit. "So wet already," he groaned as he rubbed it in little circles while she worked his dick. The pressure started building like an inferno in her middle she gripped the tops of his thighs and opened her throat taking him all the way back. It felt so good, the invasion in her mouth, while his fingers worked her. His rumbling growl of pleasure was enough to send her racing over the edge and she came in a rush all over his hand.

She was intent on finishing him too when he pulled her mouth off him and pushed her back into the cushions. Climbing on top of her he settled in the opening of her thighs, pushing them further apart with his weight. The head of his dick was right at her entrance and she was still pulsing from her orgasm. Instead of pushing right in like she expected he reached down and unsnapped her bra freeing her breasts. Leaning down he took her pouty pink nipple into his mouth and sucked hard. Undone, on a gasp she rocked her hips up taking him in. He gripped her hands and held them over her head. Still working her nipple in his mouth, not moving his hips. His dick was big, there was a moment of pain, since she had never been so full before, until her body adjusted to him.

"Impatient Kay, I was gonna go slow, I didn't want to hurt you." He shook his head.

"I just want to feel you, Lex, I don't need slow." She was growling now. Moving her hips as much as she could with his pressing her down. Lifting his head up and looking into her eyes he seen the truth of it. He lifted his hips pulling all the way out, and pushed swiftly back in. At her gasp he did it again. Then he was just as lost as she was, their bodies making a slick sound as he rocked in and out of her. The pressure was building already, and Kayla was gasping for breath. "Shit, Lex, I'm gonna come again," she whispered raggedly.

He moved one hand down to her hips held her in place as he plundered. Pushing in and out of her faster and faster, still gripping her hands in the other. All the colors in the room seemed to coalesce into a blinding white light. As her body strung up tight like a bow Kayla closed her eyes, and cried out pulsing around him. He was grunting now too, and when she could open her eyes again, he looked glorious. His eyes blazing silver, jaw clenched breath coming in quick pants, he was almost feral. She felt his dick swell impossibly bigger and then he was pulling out and reaching down he shot warmth all over her stomach. Never before had the sight of a man in the throes of orgasm looked so perfect to her.

Neither one of them said anything, as he stared down at her huffing breath for a few moments. Locked in each other's eyes, lost in what they had just done. When the stickiness on her started cooling he broke the connection and got up, walked into the kitchen grabbed a washcloth and brought it back. He cleaned her so very gently. "I should have grabbed a condom, but we moved so quick that I didn't think of it," he said. She nodded her head. When she didn't say anything he followed with, "I don't want you thinking I invited you over here for this." He set the washcloth on the floor, folded just so, and sat back down looking at her.

Suddenly it was all too much for her. She couldn't listen to what he was going to say, didn't want to give him the chance to push her away. So she went on the defense. "No big deal. Ah, it's late, I have to work both jobs tomorrow." Pulling on only her sweater and grabbing everything else making a pile in her arms. "But hey, thanks for scratching my itch. Dry spell over. I will catch you later." And she ran out leaving him still sitting on the couch staring after her.

Chapter 4

The sound of his side door slamming had Lex dropping his head in his hands, as it echoed through the small house. Wondering out loud to himself what the hell just happened? Kayla thanked him for scratching an itch, like they hadn't just got caught in a whirlwind and devoured each other as if they were half starved. *'Oh, by the by, thanks for banging me senseless.'* Seriously? Meanwhile Lex's hands were literally trembling, being with Kayla had done that, and he stared at them for a few minutes trying to will them into stillness.

An entire decade of strictly self-enforced distance from her flew right out the window scant minutes after she walked into his house. Had he really thought he could exorcise her from his system if he just ignored the fire in his blood for her? That made him the biggest idiot ever he supposed. She wasn't supposed to be his. Oh, he knew she had always had a crush on him growing up. He used to think it was cute for the longest time. She was his best friend's, his brother in all ways but blood, baby sister. That put her firmly in the do not ever touch category.

Then one day, looking back, she outgrew the pig tails and scuffed knees. And he suddenly found himself getting lost in the way her eyes sparkled when she laughed. He was noticing how firm and perky her tits were under her shirt. Then night after night he was having wet dreams about what she would taste like, the feel of her moving under him. His resolve was growing weak. Eating sandwiches, nobody else around, just the two of them, he just soaked her in like the vibrant light she was. Willpower destroyed, in a moment of weakness, he tried so hard to hate himself for, he kissed her. And he felt it. That spark racing from her into him. Damn it, damn it, damn it. Kayla was his fated mate! Struggling to process that he ran out of her parent's kitchen as if his feet had wings. It had stunned him. Burned straight down into his soul.

Now a decade later he was the one left staring after her as she ran from him. Lex figured he definitely one hundred percent deserved it. It was all that kept him from chasing after her. That didn't mean it didn't gut him knowing being with him like that freaked her out and had her running away. Nothing he could do about it now. His hands finally done shaking, he took a deep breath and bent over and picked up the washcloth filled with his jizz and brought it into the bathroom. Rinsing it out before he tossed it into the hamper. What an idiot he was, for thinking he could just talk to her. He was feeling like a jerk all night, that look on her face as she had laid into him in the parking lot. Then picturing her with another guy, and her angry speech playing in the background on repeat. Looking at himself in the mirror he called himself an idiot. There was no going back from this now. He knew what her body felt like, pulsing around him, the way she sounded as she came. He saw her eyes as they shattered. No other woman would ever be able to satisfy even the most physically basic of needs now. Wondering how the hell he was ever going to make it right, he hopped in the shower. As much as his wolf loved her smell all over him, he knew that he needed the cool water to help him think. Later as he lay in bed, he decided that he was going to woo her. Hopefully convince her to give him a real shot, and this time, he wasn't going to waste it.

***

Early the next morning Lex texted Kian asking him to stop by before heading into work. This time he was going to come clean about all of it with her brother. Kian texted back letting him know he could be over in a few. This could go very wrong, but if he wanted to be with Kayla he needed Kian to understand. Drinking coffee to settle his nerves he watched out the window for his best friend. "It's open," he yelled as Kian walked up. "Hey Deck. Can we talk?" he asked, using the nickname he always called Kian.

"Is this about the search for my uncle, or about you kissing my baby sister ten fucking years ago?" Kian asked looking annoyed.

"I take it she told you." Lex noticed his Alpha's eyes remained blue, no silver. So the man was annoyed, but the wolf wasn't out for blood. Yet.

"Yeah man. She told me all of it yesterday. What happened, and how it broke her into jagged little pieces. That my Dad knew and convinced her you would come around as soon as you worked it out in your head." Kian walked into Lex's kitchen and poured himself a cup of coffee.

"Mick knew?" Lex asked, surprised.

"Yeah, I guess she confided in him while she was figuring out whether to skin your hide for running off." Kian drank a sip of his coffee. "My Dad really liked you, man, and he thought you might be good enough for his daughter. Which is why I'm not going to kick your ass for kissing my sister. But why did you run away? You broke Kayla's heart, man."

"Because I felt it, Deck. And it scared the living hell out of me. I was only twenty, still young enough to be dumb. Here's my mate, holy fucking hell, and she is my best friend's baby sister. I thought I would lose you, and it would mean losing her too. I was going to make it right, and then Mick died in that accident, and I just didn't want to add more shit to the weight on your shoulders. After the ragged edge of his loss dulled a little I convinced myself that she didn't feel the buzz between us. I wasn't about to chase after someone that wasn't mine."

"Kayla is your fated one? You're sure?" Kian looked stunned.

"Yeah, if I wasn't sure ten years ago I damn sure am now." Lex couldn't help but glance at the couch. He ended up opening the windows last night to air her scent out it because it was driving his wolf crazy.

"You need to explain."

"I felt like a right bastard for what happened at Decker Construction yesterday. So I called her meaning to apologize, and invited her over for some reason instead. I guess I was hoping I could explain, and maybe clear the air between us, tell her I hope I hadn't ruined her date. I want her happy, we have to live in the same small pack, ya know. We're sitting here having a beer and she starts going on about how it was okay, I didn't ruin anything because the guy never had a chance. He had brown hair and brown eyes, and she can't date guys that look like that since they remind her of me. That she can't get me out of her head and when they're touching and kissing her, she wishes it was me. Seriously, what the hell was I supposed to do with that, man?" Lex asked. Deck just shook his head. "I was lost, just sucked right in. I touched her face and kissed her. I meant it to be sweet, but then we fucking exploded, man. Just ignited, had to have each other. I'll spare you the details, but it was amazing. Then we're sitting there afterwards, kind of in shock just looking at each other, like we survived something monumental, and she bolts. Grabs all her clothes, thanks me for scratching her itch, and runs the hell out."

"OK, Lex, even sparing me the details that's definitely more than I ever wanted to imagine about my sister's sex life. But aside from that, it sounds like it scared her. Kinda like it did you ten years ago. And thank fucking hell it didn't go that far back then, because mate or not, if you'd done my sixteen-year-old sister I would have ripped you apart."

"I think the reason it happened the way it did was because it's been simmering between us for so long. Just so we're clear I already felt like a complete perv for kissing her, I wouldn't have done that. It's eaten me up since then as it is." Finishing his coffee, Lex rinsed the mug and set it on the sink next to the counter.

"Yeah, I can see that. So what now?" Kian checked the time on his watch.

"Kayla is my mate. I want to convince her that I am worth giving another shot. I get that I screwed it up with her. Hurt her. I want to make that right."

"OK, if she wants you, feels like you do, then you have my blessing. Both as her brother, and as your Alpha." Kian slapped Lex on the back and passed him the empty mug. While Lex rinsed it he added, "Just don't tell me any more about the sex, huh. That's not something I need to know."

"Gotcha. Thanks Deck. I'm sorry I didn't tell you sooner. Might have saved us a lot of water under the bridge."

The men headed out through the garage door. Lex heading for his cruiser, and Kian to the big black truck with Decker Construction emblazoned on the side.

With a final look at Lex before hopping in Kian said, "Things happen the way they're meant to, man. Good luck. Kayla can be pretty stubborn."

Heading into the station for his shift Lex knew Kian was right. Kayla may have been small, but she was as strong of a woman as they came. If he was going to win the rights to her heart it was going to take patience. Good thing years on the job had taught him how to hunt slowly, meticulously. Nodding to his Lieutenant he got his route for that day. It was a big county, with nine hundred and forty miles to patrol. They might not have a bustling metropolis, but there was enough to keep them busy. Fact was people out in the sticks got into just as much trouble as anywhere else.

Inspiration struck a few hours later, and Lex pulled into the small flower shop. The lady behind the counter gave him a big grin as he walked in. They had gone to high school together, and he remembered hearing that she was newly divorced. He could smell the attraction wafting off of her, and being as gentlemanly as he could he told her he was interested in sending flowers to someone very special. Her face fell a little, but she recovered quickly asking him what kind of flowers he wanted to send. "I don't know much about flowers," he admitted, "but she likes vibrancy and color."

"What about some pink Asiatic lilies, with some blue iris' nestled in for added interest?" She pointed out the different flowers.

"Those definitely look happy to me, they don't say 'friends' though, right? Men send them to their sweethearts?" Lex asked, well and truly out of his comfort zone.

"Oh, absolutely. If a man were to send me these, I wouldn't think he wanted to be friends." She gave him her best saleswoman smile.

"OK then, I'm sold." He rattled off the address they needed to go to as she handed him a little card to write his message on.

```
KAYLA,
LAST  NIGHT  WAS  THE  BEST
OF MY LIFE.
FINALLY    GETTING    TO
TOUCH YOU, WAS THE HOPE
I    HAVEN'T    ALLOWED
MYSELF  TO  DREAM  OF  ALL
THESE YEARS.
LEX.
```

Tucking the message into the envelope and sealing it he handed it back. She looked wistfully down at the card a moment before she told him the total. Taking out his wallet and handing over his debit card he asked when they would be delivered. Swiping his card and handing him the receipt she told him they would go out just after lunch. Thanking her for all of her help he walked out into a rare sight. The sun was blazing in the sky, making the snow covering the ground sparkle like crushed diamonds. February in Michigan was typically cloudy and gray. Sometimes the sun wouldn't shine for a week at a time. Soaking up the vitamin D with a smile Lex walked back to his cruiser.

Chapter 5

Emma walked into Decker Construction with a smile on her face and a bag of what smelled like Chinese takeout for lunch. Kayla glanced up as she was setting up a meeting with the realtor like Kian had asked. The half dozen houses left vacant after the battle were still in pack territory. Not wanting unsuspecting humans buying them Decker Construction was trying to put bids in for all of them as a package deal. It would definitely be a stretch, but they didn't have many other options. Setting the phone back on the hook Kayla said "Hey, that smells divine, I sure hope there is some for me."

"But of course. How about we all eat in Kian's office." Always beautiful, Emma had changed so much in the short time since Kayla had known her. She used to have one foot out the door at all times. Born a shifter without a wolf, she had never been able to settle down. She's really blossomed here though. The love between her and Kian shone bright as the sun. Not to mention Kayla herself had given Emma a wolf of her own now. There was always a glint in her golden green eyes now. Like she had gone so long without a wolf that she couldn't ever tuck her in completely. Not having to regret turning Emma brought a smile to Kayla's face.

"How does it feel to be back working?" Kayla asked. Emma was a nurse at the clinic in town, but after threats against her life she had to stop going into work for a while for everyone's safety.

"Great. I was going crazy cooped up at home. I'm sure everyone appreciated being able to get back to their lives too, after putting so much time into watching me."

"Shut it. It's not like we were babysitting, Em, and it wasn't a chore. We look out for our own. Besides, I like hanging out with you, silly." Kayla gave Emma's curly auburn pony tail a gentle tug.

"But, now I can bring you lunch, that's a nice perk right?" Emma laughed leading the way down the hall. It definitely was a nice perk indeed.

Emma walked over to Kian and gave him a kiss before setting the food down. Expecting no less Kayla settled in a chair to wait it out. Fated mates were never shy with their affection, the wolves inside just wouldn't allow it. Emma got them what looked like enough food for two times as many people. Shifters ate more than an average human, it just took more calories for their bodies to function. Controlling the wolf inside, or changing from one form to another was a lot of work. There were heaping cartons of sweet and sour chicken, beef with broccoli, orange chicken, dumplings, noodles, rice, egg rolls, and Kayla's personal favorite crab Rangoon. Emma had grabbed some paper plates, and plastic silverware on the way here also. Once her brother and his mate came up for air Kayla started divvying up the food on the plates.

In between bites Emma said, "So I hear Lex got you flowers." Kayla glared at both of them silencing Kian's laugh. His shoulders were shaking though.

"Yeah, you would think he never had sex before. Flower delivery the next morning, he brought me lunch the day after that, and this morning he dropped off coffee, fancy coffee. I mean, yeah the sex was good, really really good, but jeez." Kayla shoved a dumpling in her mouth looking annoyed.

"If it bugs you so much why do you keep the flowers on your desk?" Kian pointed out. "I saw you looking at them with a goofy look on your face too."

"Well, it's not the flowers fault. And I like flowers," Kayla told her brother, her tone suggesting the 'duh' was implied.

"They're lovely Kayla, it was perceptive of him not to go with the standard red roses," Emma added.

"Well, everyone knows I like color," Kayla shrugged with a sigh, admitting, "Of course I like them, wish he hadn't sent them, but I might as well enjoy them since he did."

"Maybe being with you really meant a lot to him. I think he wants a second shot." Emma looked over at her mate Kian, "Did he say anything to you babe?"

"Oh, come on! I can't answer that. It's against every guy code there is. What he told me in confidence stays between us." Kian reached for seconds as Emma shook her head at him.

"I just don't know that I can give him a chance. It hurt so bad the first time, why would I ask for that again?" Kayla said looking down at her plate.

"You two shared one kiss back then, and look how long that has affected you. Sleeping together is so much bigger. Besides, how are you going to feel if he eventually gives up and moves on? Have you thought of that? Your lives are so connected that it's going to be impossible to escape that unless one of you leaves. I don't want to lose either of you, I just got you," Emma said softly. Kayla just shook her head and couldn't bring herself to answer.

"If you want to talk about it, share all the juicy deets, or if you need a shoulder you know to come to me, okay? Alright, I'm changing the subject now, you can take a breath. How has it been going working both jobs?"

"I like it here, didn't realize how much I missed it I guess. It isn't too bad working with bossy ass Kian," Kayla scrunched her nose at him. "They hired two new waitresses' at Dusty's to help cover shifts. So I don't feel like I am leaving them in the lurch which is good. I used to like going in to work every day, I mean, it was fun and I was good at it. I always like the controlled chaos. But I find I am dreading it now. I guess maybe the appeal of drunk guys grabbing your ass and asking for your number wears off." Kayla got up tossing her empty plate in the trash. "Thanks for lunch Emma, I have to get back out there, I'm trying to reorganize the filing system. Some of it's a real mess."

Kayla shut the door on her way out of the office giving herself some space. She could still hear them talking low, but it helped her to block it out. Her mind was a jumble lately. She kept replaying what happened with Lex. The sex was incredible, like none she ever had before. If that was all there was between them she could have happily gone back for more and more. It wasn't just sex though. Never would be. This was Lex, the same guy she's harbored feelings for ever since she discovered the appeal of guys during puberty. She couldn't have stopped it though, caught up in the heat bouncing between them that magnifying until it burst into flames. Once she came down from the high, she felt exposed, her soul just split wide open. Not sure if she should show him her heart Kayla had booked it out of there and cried the whole way home. Kole had been asleep when she got in thankfully because a weeping sister wouldn't have been something he could ignore as none of his business.

Kayla was still trying to close the door inside locking him back out again. It was easier wrapping herself in the snarky attitude she had before. Then he sent her flowers, beautiful, thoughtful flowers. With a note that she tucked away behind the cards in her wallet. He called her his hope. Why couldn't she have been his hope years ago? What changed now? Getting annoyed at herself Kayla shook her head and got back to work.

Kian left with Emma a few minutes later. He was heading to the job site to help out Kole and Jase for the rest of the afternoon. Happy to be left alone with the task at hand Kayla dug through more of the random files. Paperwork should be organized by category, year, and then alphabetically within each year. Most of it was just categorically filed, but that's as far as it got. Once you got to where you needed to look a lot of time was wasted digging through for what you needed. It wasn't so disorganized when she helped out in high school, but that was ten years ago. Maybe Cathy got lazy as time went on? She might have been able to put her finger to any file she needed in a moment's notice, but it was taking Kayla longer than it needed to.

Kayla was fully immersed in forms and files hours later when the phone rang. Picking it up on autopilot she said, "Good afternoon, Decker Construction, how may I assist you?"

"Kayla? Hello niece of mine. I read about the fire. How very...tragic. I suppose that means that

Kian has taken the pack well in hand," her uncle Russ said. Kayla blinked in shock for a moment.

Recovering quickly Kayla replied with a vicious snarl, "You didn't leave much choice did you dear Uncle? Why are you calling, there is nothing left for you. If you show your face here again I will gladly rip it off."

"You could try," Russell Decker laughed as he hung up.

Kayla let out a terrifying growl fighting the wolf that wanted to tear out of her skin. It wasn't the time or the place. Taking deep breaths Kayla stood up bracing her hands on the desk. After a few minutes her wolf had settled marginally. Knowing that was as much ground as she was going to gain she picked up her cell, dialing Dusty's. Carl the bartender picked up on the third ring. "Dusty's Roadhouse."

"Hey Carl, its Kayla. I'm not going to be able to make it in for my shift tonight."

"Why not? You still have an hour until you're supposed to be here," Carl said.

She knew he was counting down because then he could take a break for the rest of the night. "I'm sorry, I ah, think I had some bad Chinese for lunch. You're just going to be waiting on my tables every time I run to the lady's room to throw up," Kayla lied.

"Oh yuck, thanks for that mental picture. I'll just call one of the new girls in. Do you work tomorrow?" he asked sounding completely grossed out.

"Yeah, I was supposed to. Can you find someone to cover that too? This is really bad," Kayla added, doing her best to sound nauseated.

"Yeah, yeah, feel better," he said hanging the phone up.

With that taken care of Kayla picked up her purse, walked into the back, grabbed her coat, powered down her computer, and shut the lights off to leave. She had just locked the door and engaged the security system when the county sheriff's cruiser pulled into the parking lot. Cursing under her breath at his damn timing Kayla walked over to his car.

"What are you doing here Deputy Kolter?" She was not in the mood for another one of his gestures right now.

"Lex," he implored.

Shaking her head she waited for him to continue.

"I wanted to see if you were working tonight, and if not take you out to dinner. You know Kay, if you don't want to call me Lex, Alex works too." He gave her a big flirty grin.

"I was supposed to work, but I called in. How about you grab some pizza's and head over to my place? I was just about to text everyone."

"What's up?" The smile faded, and his eyes sharpened making a sweep of the parking lot.

He managed to look even better when he was on high alert. Sighing to herself at what a fool she was, "I will fill everyone in together. I'm OK though, you don't need to worry Lex," she couldn't help herself from adding.

"Okay, okay. I'll see you there in twenty." He waited until she got in her sport utility vehicle and followed her out on to the road.

At the stop light she pulled her phone out and called Kian. "Meeting at my house, something came up. Lex is grabbing pizzas. Can you let everyone know? I'm driving." When her brother said he would handle it she hung up and drove out of town heading home.

She had barely let herself into the house when Kole came barreling through the door. Rushing to her he grabbed her by the shoulders and looked her over. "I'm okay, Kole, it was a phone call. But I love you for worrying." She raised her hand up to cover one of his. He nodded his head, the wild silver in his eyes dimming a little. Her brothers might annoy her to no end, but she knew how much they loved her. Jase was the next one in, backwards ball cap on covering his hair. Kian walked in with his arm around Emma who looked freaked out but ready to let the wolf have her at a moment's notice. Lex walked in arms loaded down with a stack of hot and ready quick pick-up pizzas.

Once everyone was sitting down at the farmhouse style table she loved so much, Kayla told them about the phone call she received. "Russ called the office. He said that he had heard about the tragic fire. And he guessed that meant Kian was able to get the pack under him. I told him that he hadn't left us with much choice, but that if he wanted to come back I would be willing to rip him to pieces. He said that I could try and hung up still laughing to himself."

Emma spoke up, "It doesn't sound like he knew who was going to pick up." She looked over at Kian. "Almost like he didn't believe it about the fire."

"Or maybe he wasn't sure who died in it? The papers only listed the area, and that there were multiple victims. No names," Jase said.

"I didn't think about that, but it makes sense," Kole added. "What if he called expecting Cathy to answer and when it wasn't her he just winged it?"

"It's possible. The names were kept out of the paper in case we managed to track down any relatives. They would need to be notified before names were released." Lex looked at Kayla. "You said he was laughing, how else did he sound?"

"Well I was pretty focused on the files I was trying to sort through when I answered the phone. He snapped me out of it quickly though. It seems like he was fishing looking back on it. But if it had gone the other way that day, wouldn't Cathy or someone called him back letting him know? Maybe he has been waiting for that."

"I think that's the way of it. He hadn't heard from Cathy, and he was double checking before heading back here. The fire could just have easily been at one of our places. And he was hoping that was the case. Now that he knows it wasn't we are going to have to be on guard. I don't put anything past him at this point," Kian said with eyes swirling into silver. "Let him try and take this pack from me," adding on a growl.

Chapter 6

This wasn't exactly the way he wanted the evening with Kayla to go. Lex would have preferred to take her out to eat, or even cook for her, just the two of them. An emergency pack meeting was far from the romantic atmosphere he was hoping for. Nevertheless, it was time he got to spend near Kayla. She looked pissed off, and stressed out, but still so beautiful it left his hands a little shaky. She had on dark jeans with a teal button-down blouse. It was slightly sheer, and he could see the lace edged camisole she was wearing underneath it. There was a slim head band placed in her hair, Lex figured just for looks since it wasn't holding anything back. She arranged the hair towards her face, with a deep side part. There were little silver dangles hanging from her ears, and a stack of bracelets on her arm that tinkled when she moved. Kayla always looked exciting, and spontaneous, to him. Like she was always ready for an adventure and was determined to bring some color along with her.

Her deep brunette hair used to be much longer, but she cut it short not too long ago. The effect was playful, and sexy leaving nothing to distract from her face. Large steel blue eyes framed with long dark lashes. Her slim nose turned up ever so slightly at the tip. She had a mouth that was constantly moving. Whether it be laughing, talking, singing along, or pursed and scowling. And, hoping he was the only one that paid enough attention to notice, but she bit the side of her bottom lip just before an orgasm ripped through her. And her smell, he could never get over the way she smelled of warmth and spice, nothing he could put a finger on, just mysteriously sexy. Kayla brought life everywhere she went, and he was finally willing to admit that his life without her these long years had been drained of joy.

Lex, not ready to leave yet, stayed behind as the others all said their goodbyes. "How about I help clean up?" he asked.

"Since I'm on cleanup for the month it won't earn you entrance into my panties tonight big boy," Kole joked with wiggly eyebrows and kissy faces at him.

"Honestly Kole, like loading the dishwasher is the same as open sesame when it comes to my panties. Besides, mind your own business ya creep." Kayla tossed her napkin at him as she got up from the table.

"OK, that wasn't exactly what I meant guys," Lex added a little embarrassed. "I wasn't aiming for anyone's panties."

"So, you don't want to fuck my sister?" Kole asked with his head in the refrigerator loading the leftover pizza boxes inside.

"Shit Kole. There isn't a right answer there. I say I want to sleep with her and it will seem like that's all I want, and if I say no I'm not interested in sex and everyone here will know I'm lying. How about I stick with, I wasn't ready to go home yet Kayla, can I keep you company for a while more?"

Lex said all exasperated while Kole cackled with laughter.

"Nope. I'm going to go up, and I don't want company in bed," Kayla said with a scowl as she walked up the stairs.

Lex was shaking his head and standing to leave when Kole said, "She needs time. She spent so long denying there was anything between you that it's hard for her to stop that now. Besides, I bet she is afraid you're going to change your mind once she goes all in on this."

"She wasn't the only one locking everything inside Kole. It's all I've been doing for the last ten years too. I wasn't trying to hurt her. I know I did, but that wasn't my intent. It's all fucked up now, and I just want to fix it so I can be the man in her life. But I don't know if I can fix it," Lex said staring dejectedly up at the ceiling listening to the sound of Kayla walking around her room readying for bed.

"Well, if she didn't want you she wouldn't have had sex with you. I guess it will just take time for her to come around to the rest of it. Don't tell her

I told you this, but she fell asleep on the couch the other day, and she said your name in her sleep," Kole whispered.

"Really? My name? I wonder if it was a good dream, or a bad one?" Thinking with so much history between them it could be either one. "Thanks man, are you going out this weekend?"

"Yeah, but I figured I would see if Jase wanted to come along, that way should shit hit the fan we could handle it. He could probably use a distraction too. I know it was harder on him than us, choosing Kian. He knows he made the right choice and all, but it was never even a decision for the rest of us," Kole said pouring them each two fingers of whiskey into glasses.

Taking the drink from Kole Lex sighed. "There is more going on than we realize Kole. I can feel it, makes the hairs on the back of my neck stand up. Like the messy files Kayla was talking about? Cathy didn't tolerate mess at all. Something isn't right with that."

"I know. Just not sure what it means yet. Maybe instead of trying to find Russ, you should go back? See if there is anything in his history? It's strange, he's my uncle and all, but I don't think I ever knew him now. Alpha challenges, brawling for rank, that's expected in a pack. I always figured he and Kian would duke it out sooner or later, but I had no idea that he was a slimy bastard. Makes you wonder what else he has been hiding," Kole said throwing back the glass, emptying it quickly.

Lex mulled it over as he drove home. Kole was right. Made sense for there to be more skeletons in the closet so to speak. Russell Decker was a man who enjoyed the power he held over other people, a man that saw himself above reproach. Was he corrupted by being Alpha, or did he strive for that position because it gave him the outlet he needed? There weren't any older pack members anymore. Some had moved on to other areas, and the rest were gone. He needed to get as clear of a picture of who their previous leader was when he was a young man. Deciding that the quickest route was to call his parents. That meant letting them in on the secret of Emma's parents. But it was past time, and Lex knew he wasn't going to be able to keep that from them for long anyway. Since he had the day off tomorrow, he grabbed a beer, turned his computer on, and called his folks. Figuring since it was only nine o'clock, they would still be awake. Knowing he was right when they answered on the third ring.

"Alexander my boy! Is everything alright honey?" his Mom greeted him. She was still a lovely woman in her mid-fifties' who taught elementary school. She was soft and loving, but she had a spine of steel and Lex adored her.

"I'm okay, Mom. Is Dad close by?" Lex asked. "I have a lot to tell you the both of you."

"Yeah, I'm here son. You told us all about the upheaval in the pack, are there more problems? We can come up there if there is a need," his father said turning the phone on speaker.

"No, you're good where you are. But I left some details out when I told you what happened with the pack, and Kian being Alpha."

"Sounds like maybe you should fill us in then," his Mom said.

"Okay, let me get it all out at once okay? I told you that Kian met his mate? Well she was the catalyst for this entire thing. She didn't know it though. Emma, that's her name, she was born without a wolf to shifter parents." He could hear his mother's surprise, and his father gently shushing her. "Russell Decker wasn't too keen on letting her in the pack. He caused a bit of a stink and then took off on what he said was a quick business trip. Then Emma got a call threatening her life, and telling her that there was a lot she didn't know about her past. Kian asked me to look into it unofficially, and I found some seriously bad stuff. First of all, you need to know that we kept her safe. It turns out that her parents were Patrick and Beth Lowe, formerly MaryBeth Kolter."

"My MaryBeth's girl?" his Dad said sounding all choked up. "We haven't heard anything from her in so many years."

"I'm sorry to tell you this Dad, but she was killed in a car accident when Emma was a toddler. Her Dad must have suspected the same thing I do, that it wasn't an accident, someone forced her off the road on purpose, killing her." He could hear his mother crying now. Hating that this was hurting them he went on. "Patrick moved Emma around a whole lot for the next ten years, homeschooling her. When she was twelve, he finally put her back in public school, in Georgia, I think to keep her safe because he knew running wasn't working. When she came home from school one day he was gone. She always believed he took off on her, that's what the police at the time told her. She went into the foster care system then. Fast forward many years and she takes a job in town here as a nurse at the clinic. Kian meets her, and he realizes they're fated to be mates. While I was digging into the threat on her life I found out that the body of what is most likely her father was discovered a few years after he disappeared. It was a state away in the middle of the forest."

"That poor girl. Does she know that she is related to you Alex?" his mother asked.

"You said she didn't have a wolf?" his father added.

"Yeah, she knows. I should have seen it sooner; she looks just like the pictures of MaryBeth I've seen. Except instead of brown eyes, she has these golden green ones, she said they were like her fathers. We have been getting to know each other as cousins. I really like her, and of course she is perfect for Kian."

"Fate never gets that wrong," his mother interrupted.

"I know. Back to what I was saying, she didn't have a wolf, but her senses were all heightened like ours. During the battle Cathy Wyles and her husband meant to kill her, thinking that was what Russ would have wanted. Kayla got there in time to halt their original attack, but she couldn't hold them off forever. So Kayla bit Emma. Thinking that even if it killed her it was better than the way she would be going if the Wyles' got to her. It didn't though, thankfully, she turned. And she is a pretty big bad ass. Newly turned and she was fighting next to her mate."

"What color is she?" his Dad asked him, sounding a little gruff from the emotions running through him.

"Ah, her wolf is a russet color," Lex answered him.

"Just like her mother. MaryBeth's wolf was a beautiful red, just like her hair. A heart of gold, that one, but she didn't take any crap," Lex's father said.

"I didn't think about that at all. Emma wants to get to know you. She grew up without a family, and is a little nervous, but she still willing to give it a shot. Okay, anyway, Kayla has been working in the office of Decker Construction, and she got a call from her uncle today. We think he was trying to see what was going on in the pack, just sniffing around. She told him she would rip his face off if he showed back up here, he laughed and said she could try."

"Oh, I bet she could. Kayla was always a force to be reckoned with, like a hurricane when she was little," his mother added.

"Yeah, but it got us thinking that maybe there was more dirt Russell Decker has been hiding, and that's got me looking into his past. And actually, one of the reasons I called you. What was he like before he was an Alpha. Did it corrupt him, or was he always twisted?" Lex finished. So much for getting it all out at once with no interruptions.

"He wasn't the nicest of boys when he was young. Always into some trouble, and not the good-natured stuff. His father was always fixing things for him, which was probably part of the problem. Old man Decker picked his younger son as a favorite early on, and everyone knew it. Mick grew up to be a good man, didn't have a chip on his shoulder where most probably would. But when Mick found Hannah and they started having babies, I think Russ hated him for it. He hadn't found a true mate, and my sister MaryBeth didn't want him. I don't think Mick ever really seen it, Russ hid it from him so well. And he didn't come out and say it, but I saw the way he looked at his older brother when he thought nobody was looking. There was so much jealousy and hatred there. So, to answer your question son, I would go back as far as you can when digging into Russell Decker's closet," his Dad answered.

Knowing his parents had a lot to absorb now, and would need to talk it over between the two of them Lex told them he loved them, and that he would call them soon, before ending the call. It made a sick kind of sense to Lex now, thinking like a cop. The reason that Russ couldn't get over his aunt MaryBeth was because he never learned how to take the answer no. He got what he wanted, and he thought the world owed it to him. When his aunt had denied Russ, and then run off with another man, it wasn't something he could get past. Mick and Hannah having Kian, Kole, and then Kayla only added fuel to that raging hatred. Russ was a much sicker man than Lex originally thought. Logging into his work account Lex was dreading what he was going to find buried in the past.

Chapter 7

After spending most of the night tossing and turning Kayla was in a right nasty mood. Pissed off for letting herself wonder what could be with her and Lex. She spent an entire hour picturing what kind of future they could have in a perfect world. Then she regretted every bit of it when it left her with a deep longing for what might never be. Giving up on sleep and calling herself all kinds of foolish she decided to go on a run. Not as a wolf, no, but the kind where you lace up some shoes and get lost in the pounding of your feet against the pavement. There hadn't been any snow fall in a few days, so the roads were clear. It was still below freezing outside, but that was a Michigan winter for you. Being a shifter Kayla was perfectly warm in the compression leggings, support tank top, fleece half zip and a beanie over her hair. Normally when Kayla needed to run it out, she blasted dance music through her headphones. The pulsing beat and sexual rhythm made the miles less tedious. This morning though she needed the silence, there was too damn much mucking up her head already. When she'd passed Lex's house on her way out it was completely dark still. Which had only pissed her off further, how dare he sleep soundly when he was keeping her up! Kayla ran for a few miles before looping around to head back. She was watching the dawn break over the trees, as she approached Lex's place. She noticed a light flick on. *Our mate is awake* her wolf said. Before Kayla could even attempt to stop herself she was running up his driveway and banging on his damn door.

Lex opened the door in nothing but a pair of blue plaid boxers. His brown hair was waving in all different directions. There was even a crease across his shoulder from his sheets still. His melted chocolate eyes had the hazy unfocused look of sleep. "This changes nothing between us Kolter," she said before leaping up into his arms. Though barely awake, he caught her easily, and without hesitation, just like she knew he would. Her mouth was devouring his like a woman long starved as he backed into the house and kicked the door shut. Gripping the hair at the back of his head in her fists she held on as he walked her down the hall to his bedroom. The heat between them ignited just like it had the first time, and Kayla was already desperate for him by the time he sat her down next to his bed. Whipping her fleece and tank top up and over her head she tossed them aside. As soon as the air hit her skin his hands were on her aching breasts, his thumbs brushing over her sensitive nipples as he gripped them. She pulled her feet out of the shoes using the heel of the other foot for leverage. Then shoving her leggings down she hop kicked out of them in a rush to have him inside of her.

"What time do you have to be to work today?" Lex asked, his voice still gravelly from sleep.

"Soon," was all she said as she backed up towards the bed, intent on climbing up on it. He had a different idea though, and dropped to his knees in front of her. At the first touch of his tongue across her seam Kayla's head fell back. He ran his hands up the back of her legs and held her against his face she opened her legs to give him better access. Stroking her clit side to side with the flat of his tongue had her heart racing and gasping for breath. Throwing one arm behind her on the bed to help keep her standing, Kayla gripped the hair on the top of his head with the other hand. When her legs started to shake he changed the angle of his head and pushed his tongue into her on a deep rumbling growl. His tongue working in and out of her had her hips bucking desperately against him. As the first pulses of her orgasm hit, his tongue disappeared, just as she whimpered he sucked her clit into his mouth and her legs finally gave way.

Lex held on to her though, and laid her gently down on the bed. His eyes never left hers as he pushed his boxers down, freeing his hard length. "You taste much better than the coffee I was planning on making to wake me up," he said gripping his dick, his fist working it slowly. The sight of Lex stroking himself had Kayla biting her lip on a moan. His eyes glowing silver, muscles flexing and straining. Never had she seen someone look so sexy. When he climbed up onto the bed Kayla opened her legs in invitation for him, but he gripped her hips and rolled them over instead. "Want to watch you take me Kay," he said with a shake of his head.

Straddling him, her hands on his chest, eyes still on him she rotated her hips in a slow circle working his dick until it slid just barely inside of her. Moving barely up and down she rode just the head until he was panting, and she was dripping down his length. Smiling down at him like a goddess who knew her own power she pushed down hard, taking all of him inside. He was so big, her body had to stretch to take all of him. Bringing her knees up she planted her feet on the side of his hips, and pushing down on his chest she lifted her body up and down hard and fast, taking him so much deeper in this position. Breasts bouncing with the rhythm she set he was grunting with each slap of her body on his. The pressure in her middle was building, and moaning she rode him like a woman possessed. Racing him to completion. When her pussy clenched, gripping his dick with the first pulse of her orgasm he sat up and gripping her hips rocked her against him as fast as he could. Kayla's head fell back on a scream as her orgasm raged on. Lex growled into her neck, scraping his teeth against the skin as he swelled impossibly bigger and came inside of her in sporadic spurts of warmth.

Lex collapsed back on the bed taking Kayla with him. Their bodies still connected. She lay there on top of him trying to remember how to breathe. Her wolf was rejoicing inside. *Our mate almost claimed us.* Telling herself it was just the heat of the moment, and it didn't mean what her wolf wanted it to, Kayla looked up into his eyes. They were still blazing silver, like her own. No man had ever brought the silver out in her eyes until Lex. Wondering if that meant she could let herself go to fully enjoy it, or simply because nobody else had worked her body quite like Lex. Either way she was in a much better mood now than when she left the house this morning. She climbed off him with a satisfied stretch. Her muscles were gloriously loose.

Kayla was already pulling her clothes back on when Lex asked what she wanted for breakfast. "No time, I gotta get to work." He had one muscular arm tucked behind his head and she brushed a hand through his messy hair. Laying a smacking kiss on his lips she said, "this is all I can give."

"It's enough, for now. At least you didn't run out this time," he said. "Want a ride back home?"

"Nah, I'll walk. See ya later Lex," Kayla said as she walked out.

Thinking her day was looking up already, Kayla jogged the short distance home with a grin on her face. That man knew his way around her body, that was for sure. Nothing she imagined, and she spent so many nights touching herself and imagining, was even close to reality. Finally admitting to herself that just maybe a sixteen-year-old Kayla wouldn't have been able to handle everything simmering between them. Lex had probably made the right call putting a stop to it a decade earlier. He could have handled it better, but then again, it was probably all very overwhelming for him too. She was starting to see that decision had cost him a great deal too. However, that didn't mean she was quite ready to give her heart to him again. Being young and naive the last time got it crushed. *If anyone was worth the risk, its him,* her wolf reminded her. With nothing to argue that point Kayla shook her head to quiet the wolf inside and walked into her house.

"What up, sis! Felt like making breakfast burritos this morning." Kole said waving with a spatula, and turning his head with a sniff, "unless you already ate after your morning booty call?" he laughed at her.

"Nope, no food. Just amazing sex. Try not to be jealous of how many orgasms I had," Kayla said snagging a burrito and taking a giant bite. Kole didn't do it often, but he could really cook.

"I am going out tonight, where I will undoubtedly find a woman to give me many orgasms too. Besides, you're not supposed to brag about that with your brother. It's weird," Kole said shaking his head.

"What? Like we're supposed to pretend I don't enjoy sex just because I happen to be your sister? Besides, you brought it up, dumb ass," Kayla said finishing her breakfast. "Whatever girl you bang tonight will be someone's sister."

"Okay, okay. My bad. I'm glad you're happy with your sex life. Let's just leave it at that," he said holding his hands up in surrender.

Kayla laughed all the way up the stairs and into the shower.

Chapter 8

Laying in bed with a giant smile on his face Lex thought morning sex with Kayla was something he could definitely get used to. Hell, he would take it anytime of the day she felt like it. He wasn't an innocent, there were a few women he had slept with, and he had thought it satisfying, even pretty great. Until now that is. That sex completely paled in comparison to what he had with Kayla. Nothing had ever felt so good or been so intense. Just remembering the look on her face, and the sound she made as she came was making him hard again. He took it as a good sign that she hadn't run screaming for the hills this time. She had laid on top of him, her sweet body pressed against his chest. Their hearts slowing to normal together. That was damn near cuddling. Maybe next time she would stay and they could spend all day rolling around in bed discovering everything about each other.

Because Lex knew no matter how many times they had each other nothing was going to sate the hunger.

Getting up he walked into the bathroom he turned on the shower. He had been so close to claiming her this time, too close. His wolf was screaming it at him the whole time, and he almost gave in. It had taken all of his willpower to just scrape his teeth across the tender skin of her neck. She wasn't dumb though, and he knew it would occur to her how close he had come to actually biting, if it hadn't already. Calling himself an idiot he stepped into the hot water. Claiming someone without permission was a giant no-no. Nobody had ever tempted his wolf, and the first time with Kayla had been so shocking. Holding back now was going to take monumental effort, his wolf worked on instinct, and Kayla was their mate. But Lex knew with the reasoning and logic that eluded his animal side that if he claimed her before she asked him to it would be over. He would lose her forever. She would never forgive him for that, and rightly so. He was trying to prove she could trust her heart with him, not scare her off.

Stepping out of the shower Lex ran a towel roughly over his hair before wrapping it around his hips. He absolutely had to make some progress today, there was information his Alpha needed. He really had to focus now. Dialing down his emotions, Lex took a moment to step into what he thought of as his 'cop head space.' This was the Lex that could get the difficult shit done and knowing the drill his wolf went still inside with hyper focused precision. They worked together, his instincts giving him an advantage in dicey situations. This control was hard earned, he spent years practicing. Lex never let his emotions elicit a change, he couldn't afford to. He pulled on a faded gray t shirt that said KOLTER on the back across his shoulders, and a pair of jeans that had seen better days years ago.

Needing fuel, he quickly made himself some steak and eggs for breakfast while his computer booted up. Snagging a bottle of water from the refrigerator Lex carried his plate into his office.

Checking his information, he ate the food on auto pilot. Not many people knew that he was something of a hacker. It was a skill helpful to ensure the safety of the pack, which was what mattered to Lex. He could have worked for the FBI if all of the extensive background checks wouldn't have been such a risk. Truthfully his wolf would have hated the big city though, so he had no regrets. Searching for a current location on Russell Decker wasn't panning out. Russell was a smart man, so he had to be using another name, and Lex couldn't exactly put out an APB. As far as the human legal system went, Russell Decker would never be held accountable for his crimes. Which pissed Lex off, he took an oath to serve and protect after all. Throwing the previous Alpha in jail would only endanger the humans in proximity. Not to mention shattering the secrets around their existence. People just couldn't handle that. The pack had to take care of this on their own. The bastard could be sipping a fruity drink on the beaches of Mexico for all Lex could find. Putting himself in Russell's shoes though, he would stay close enough to be able to fuck with the Bid Woods Pack, and Kian especially. That meant he was most likely still in the Great Lakes region of the Midwest. Lex would find him, maybe not today, but sooner or later everyone slipped up. No matter how long it took, Lex was watching.

When you hit a brick wall it was time to switch gears. Letting his instincts guide him Lex pulled up all the information he could find from the accident that killed Mick Decker a decade before. Mick had taken his big truck out of state to meet up with a supplier that was having logistical difficulties at the time. It really should have been no big deal, the kind of thing Mick had done many times before. That's just who Mick was, the kind of man everyone liked immediately, responsible, dependable, but with a keen sense of humor, and just enough mischief to keep it interesting. Lex remembered being about five years old and wrestling Kian and his father on the living room floor. Mick had just as much fun as the two giggling boys climbing all over him had. His loss left a gaping hole, not just in the Decker family, but the whole pack.

Knowing that Russell had thought he successfully got away with killing Emma's mother Beth in an accident it stood to reason he would feel comfortable using the same method again. According to the file the state police had, road conditions were slick from the rain, taking a curve that he didn't know too quickly in the dark had Mick's truck going off the road. It had enough momentum to roll over twice before landing on its top in a field. It stated that Mick wasn't wearing a seat belt, had been tossed around in the cab of the truck ultimately breaking his neck. A broken neck would be able to kill a shifter before any damage could be repaired. Their bodies could take a hell of a lot, but ultimately, they weren't invincible.

Since Mick had technically hydroplaned off the road there wouldn't be any skid marks. The truck was traveling on a fairly deserted stretch of road and hadn't been discovered until morning. Of course Mick's mate Hannah had felt his death and knew before the police had knocked on her door to notify her. While Russell lived alone, there wouldn't have been enough time to sneak there and back. And Lex distinctly remembered that Hannah had called Russell when she felt the mate bond sever. It's a painful moment, like half of your soul is ripped out of your body. Russell was over at his brother's house within minutes of the call. Not being there in person didn't mean that he hadn't played a part in it though. Russell could have paid someone else to run Mick off the road, if so, there might be a trail Lex could follow.

Two hours later Lex was disappointed that he couldn't find any evidence that Russell had accessed a suspicious sum of money in the time leading up until the accident, or in the weeks following. Another brick wall. Tilting his head down to his shoulders, Lex cracked his neck. That's the way it worked, you tugged strings, and sometimes there wasn't anything to be found. Getting up to take his breakfast plate to the kitchen Lex let his mind float. He rinsed his plate and grabbed an apple from the wooden bowl kept on the counter that he had made in high school shop class. Biting in he started to pace across up and down the hallway talking to himself.

'Okay, okay, okay. As the Second in the pack Mick had power. He was a big ass dominant wolf, completely fierce in a fight, but he hadn't enjoyed it the way Russell did. It's doubtful that Mick was planning on overthrowing his younger brother to be Alpha. His mate and cubs were the entire world to him. That would have risked Hannah, Kian, Kole, and Kayla. They would take his back one hundred percent. That wasn't a motive, just couldn't be. Maybe it's just as simple as hate? Russell could have sent another pack member to take care of it for him, but that had risks involved. Even with a gag order in place. No, that didn't feel right. What if taking Mick out was to eliminate the threat he could see coming years down the road? Kian changed when his Dad died. He closed up in himself and took overlooking out for the family. But before that he used to be boisterous, loud, scary dominant, and always up for anything. What if Kian was the threat all along?

What better way to keep him in line then knock him down before he even stood up in the first place? Holy mother fucking shit! Russell was scared of what Kian was growing into. He could have done it too, not at zero of course, but I remember Mick used to say his boy was meant for Alpha someday. How did he fucking do it though? He wasn't even there. But he could have called, phone records, shit! No! Would that even work?"

Running back into his office so fast he sent papers fluttering in his wake. With a few less than legal clicks on the keyboard Lex brought up Russell's phone records for ten years ago. Scanning through he found the night he needed, there was the call to Russell from Hannah, when she felt the bond sever. But, just before that there was a fifteen-minute phone call between the two elder Decker brothers. Russell called Mick. Grabbing his own cell phone off the desk where he had set it earlier, he called Kian.

"Hey man. How is the digging going?" Kian answered on the second ring.

"Ah, that's why I'm calling. I think I'm on to something. But I'm just not sure. So I need your help a second," Lex replied.

"You found him?" Kian asked, his voice sharpening.

"Not yet, this is another angle I'm working. Do you think you could give me an Alpha order over the phone?" Lex stood up and walked out to his living room.

"For what?" Kian sounded confused.

"Just tell me to do something and add some Alpha push to it. Just keep in mind I have shit to do so I can't be carrying it out all day," Lex rushed out.

"Does it even work like that Lex?" Lex could almost see the suspicious look on Kian's face.

"Just trust me, okay?" Lex said. He took a deep breath to brace himself. Listening to the sound of Kian's voice with all the focus he had.

"Drop and give me ten," Kian pushed through the phone. Without hesitation Lex immediately dropped down and did ten pushups.

Kian was listening shocked. "Well shit, that works. I didn't really think it would."

"Yeah, I wasn't sure either. It was an easy command to follow though. Didn't cost me anything. Could you order me to do something I wouldn't want to do? Maybe that would hurt me?" Lex asked.

"You want me to make you hurt yourself? That's seriously fucked up. You sure?"

"Yeah Deck, its important. Shifter healing, no worries," Lex said. He trusted Kian as both a lifelong brother to him, and as his Alpha.

"Okay Lex, I need you to cut your hand. Across the palm. Right now." Kian added as much power as he could.

Lex walked into the kitchen and opening a drawer he grabbed a knife. He tried to fight it the whole time, but couldn't. He pressed the knife into his hand, quickly swiping it from the base of his thumb to his little finger. Blood immediately pooled into his hand. Grabbing the kitchen towel hanging by the sink he held it to the wound.

"It worked. I tried fighting it, but I couldn't. My loyalty to you runs too deep. Thanks Deck," Lex said through teeth gritted against the sting.

"Wait, you gonna tell me what the hell this was about? Other than showing me the parameters of my command, and creeping me right the fuck out?" Kian asked, clearly not happy. "I didn't enjoy that Lex."

"I know. You wouldn't because you're a good Alpha. I have to gather some things, but I think we need to call a pack meeting. I'm about to drop another bomb on Big Woods," Lex said. "Remember don't kill the messenger okay?"

"I'll let everyone know. My house tonight. Kole is gonna be pissed, he had plans with Jase to hunt some pussy down in Grand Rapids."

"This isn't something that should be put off. Believe me. See you later Deck," Lex said hanging up.

The last time they had a meeting to see what he found out things hadn't gone well. That was the night everyone found out that Russell Decker had murdered Emma's parents. That the reason her life was in danger was because her mother hadn't wanted to be a selfish man's mate. Beth chose to run off with Patrick to search for their happy ever after, and Russell just couldn't let go. He hunted the couple down for years. Forcing Beth off the road in Vermont, and catching up to Patrick in northern Georgia. Learning his uncle was responsible for so much of his mate's pain, Kian's wolf had ripped out of him in an uncontrolled shift. Emma had gone up and broke down in the shower. Knowing his words had caused such pain had crushed Lex. He had sat down in Kian's living room listening to Emma's sobbing, and Kian's howling outside vowing to bring an end to the evil that was Russell Decker. Now here they were again. Lex had more information to share with the pack, and it would change everything for everyone that mattered in his life, again.

Chapter 9

Kayla stopped off at home before heading over to her brother's house to change her clothes. As cute as the outfit she wore to work that day was, she wanted to be comfortable for the meeting. Knowing how these things went Kayla pulled on a pair of comfortable jeans, they had some rips in the legs, but she still loved them. A white spaghetti strap tank top, the no fuss kind with a built-in bra followed. Topping that with a lime green hoodie she headed downstairs. Kole walked in as she was shoving her feet into her favorite pair of gray chucks. He looked pretty annoyed that his plans for the night were canceled.

"Wanna ride over together?" she asked as he headed for his room.

"Nah, I'm gonna rinse some of this sweat off, and I'll be over in a few. This better be good." Kole had a hard time keeping his wolf in line, and he was convinced that sex helped. So every so often he went down to Grand Rapids for a weekend of bar hopping and anonymous hook ups.

"I'm sure it is, maybe you can head over to Dusty's Roadhouse afterward. I know there are always women asking about you," Kayla said from the other side of the bathroom door.

"Too complicated. I don't sleep with women I know, or that I'll see around town every day," Kole said over the sound of the running water.

"You know women are capable of having sex without attachments too," Kayla said walking away. It was pointless. Kole hadn't ever slept with anyone in town that she knew of. That didn't mean there weren't always women trying to get in his pants though.

Grabbing her phone and keys Kayla walked out to her ride. She could walk the short distance to the house her older brother shared with his mate, but Kayla figured she might not be in the best mood on her way back home after the meeting tonight. Pulling into Kian's driveway she noticed Lex was already there. Since he had the day off, he was rolling in his own personal truck, not the police cruiser. She parked behind him, and walked on in. Lex and Emma were in the kitchen with smiles on their faces while they talked. They had a lot to catch up on since finding out they were cousins. It was nice to see them making that connection to each other. Giving them a small wave, she turned toward where Kian was standing with his hands tucked into his front pockets and staring out the sliding glass doors to the woods beyond the yard. He was probably still pissed off from talking to Lex earlier, and on edge about whatever Lex had to tell them all tonight.

Kayla hadn't been trying to eavesdrop, but their office building was on the small side, and with her shifter hearing it was basically impossible for her not to hear. Lex had asked Kian to give him an Alpha order to hurt himself. Kian wasn't the kind of man who took his power lightly, and what Lex asked him to do had cost him. Standing next to her brother Kayla crossed her arms and leaned against his arm. She knew him well enough to know words wouldn't help. Not bothering to fix it she offered him silence and her support instead. After a few minutes he slung his arm over her shoulders and laid a kiss on the top of her head. They were still standing next to each other when they heard Jase pull up. Figures Kole would be the last one here tonight, as some stupid protest for his plans being ruined.

Jase walked in usual ball cap on, facing front this time, and holding up grocery bags he said, "Hey, I picked up stuff for sub sandwiches. Figured that would save Emma from feeding us all." He set the bags on the counter.

Emma graced him with a beaming smile, "You're an absolute genius Jase!" She got plates down from the cupboard. Kian walked into the kitchen to grab condiments out of the refrigerator and gave Jase a thankful slap on the back.

Kayla looked at Lex and was reminded of another time they ate sandwiches for dinner. The memory wasn't sharply painful anymore. It had dulled down somewhere toward bittersweet, with just a little stinging edge. Feeling another chink in the armor around her heart Kayla did what her wolf wanted and walked over to where Lex was still standing in the kitchen. His eyes on her he watched her walk the whole way over to him. Wrapping her arms around his neck she stood on her tippy-toes and kissed him. His arms came around her waist without hesitation and he hugged her to his body. It was a sweet uncomplicated kiss, meant only as a greeting, not to seduce. "Hi," she smiled up at him when it ended. Now whenever she thought about their first kiss in the kitchen she would remember this one too. How it had flooded her with happiness all the way down to her toes.

"Hi," he replied with a smile that reached his beautiful chocolate eyes. Lacing her fingers through his they walked out to the table where everyone was staring at them.

"Not a word," she warned them. Emma mimed locking her lips with a key, Jase just grinned, and Kian shook his head, but one side of his mouth was turned up in the barest hint of a smile.

Kole walked in then. "What'd I miss?"

"I brought food," Jase said with a wink at Kayla. Laughter broke out, everyone but Kole getting the joke.

As was the routine they finished eating their food before getting to the actual reason why they were gathered. The warm camaraderie faded, and everyone could sense it was weighing heavily on Lex. It was clear he was dreading what he had to share, and that made her not want to hear it either. Kayla wished she could clasp her hands over her ears and block whatever it was out. That wasn't the way it worked though. Lex got up and running outside a moment, he came back in with a manila folder filled with papers. The air was so heavy it was practically crackling. Everyone's wolves were tense, and the smell of fur was strong around the table. Not bothering to sit back down Lex took a deep breath, looked right into Kayla's eyes and said, "Nobody wants to hear what I found out today, any more than I want to have to say it. I wish I didn't have to."

"We know your heart Lex. It's plain to see it pains you," Emma said encouragingly.

Lex nodded his head and turned to Kian. "I called our Alpha today with a theory. I asked him to give me an order I wouldn't want to carry out. He didn't want to, but I convinced him it was important. He first told me to do some pushups. Obedience was too easy, so I asked him to make it something I wouldn't want to do. He told me to cut my hand. I tried really fucking hard to fight it, and wasn't able to, guess I'm too loyal to Deck to resist." Holding up his hand he showed everyone the fading pink line across the width of his palm. "I wasn't sure if the order would stick over the phone. Never had a reason to wonder before. But it does, with all the same strength an order face to face would. I haven't been able to locate Russell yet, though I'm not giving up, sometimes you have to come at a problem from a different angle. So I went backwards, and called my parents wondering if becoming Alpha ruined Russell, or if he was a corrupt S.O.B before that. They told me that he was the favored son of old man Decker, and grew up always feeling superior to his older brother. He never openly hated Mick, but my

Dad said that he suspected that was the way of it. When Mick found his mate in Hannah, and started having cubs, it was the first thing his father couldn't take from Mick and give to him instead. Russell tried forcing my aunt, Emma's mother, into a mate pairing. She chose another man and ran off with him instead. His inability to get what he wanted led to the senseless deaths of Emma's parents. Which got me thinking that Russell really thought he got away with it, so why not use murder as a means to get what he wanted again."

"NO! He couldn't have." Kole stood up, shaking his head in denial. "He was at the house when the cops came to tell us about Dad. No, nope, no."

Putting it together Kayla said, "The phone call to Kian. You think that he, what ordered his own brother to crash?" Her hands were balled up in fists under the table, concentrating on breathing in and out was the only thing stopping the tears from welling up behind her eyes.

"I don't know what he specifically ordered him to do. Only the two of them know what was said, one can't tell us, and the other can't be trusted. I can prove he was on the phone with him just before the accident though. If he gave your Dad an order then, he wouldn't have had a choice Kay. He was too loyal, I'm sorry. So sorry." Lex looked as gutted as she felt.

"Why? What reason would the evil bastard have for killing my father? He was a good man, my Dad was a good man. He was happy to be Second to his brother, ask anyone it didn't bother him. He wasn't a threat. Dad never would've made a play for Alpha, never." Kian walked over to lay a hand on Kole's shoulder. Kole was shaking so hard he was vibrating.

"I have no proof on this, just my instinct, but I think it was you Kian. You were the threat. Do you remember how you were before? You've always been powerful, way early too. I think your uncle was afraid you would be the end of him."

"But why kill his Dad, Lex? I'm sorry, that just doesn't make any sense to me." Emma looked over at

Kian with tears shimmering in her pretty golden green eyes.

"To knock him down a peg. Take his steady footing out from under him. That would buy Russ years," Jase said looking absolutely sickened.

"I think so, yeah. Kill your Dad, and step in as the only man for you to look up to, Kian. He thought maybe he could mold you in his image. You were always going to be Alpha, always no question. This way he was ensuring you wouldn't want to take it from him. It worked too; you didn't, you never challenged him at all until Emma came. Which is another reason for Russell to hate Emma, she woke you up to your full potential," Lex pointed out.

"So your saying that my Dad was ordered to somehow kill himself so that my brother didn't take the fucking Alpha title from my uncle?" Kole raged. "What about the rest of us? Kian wasn't the only one who lost a Dad that day!" Pushing Kian's hand off him Kole said, "I'm outta here."

"Wait Kole," Kian said with desperation.

"I can't. I know it's not your fault. Know it, but it still hurts. And he did it because he was scared of you," Kole said without turning.

"Are you coming back?" Kian asked sounding like a lost boy.

"I don't know. And don't you fucking dare order me to stay damn it!" Kole said walking out the door and into the cold night.

The remaining members of the pack sat there in stunned silence trying to absorb what happened. Kian dropped down to his knees with his head in his hands making a keening sound. Emma leaned over his back and hugged him looking shell shocked. Jase stared out the door Kole just left from. Lex stood hands braced on the dark wood of the table like it would help him support the weight of the world resting on his shoulders. Kayla lost the fight against her tears, and they flowed unchecked down her face now. She stood up from her chair, Lex looked over at her, and she was heading over to him for comfort, when the realization hit her, stopping her in her tracks. "Shit, shit, shit! Someone is going to have to call Mom, she needs to know." Knowing it was going to rip the heart right out of her mother's chest had Kayla growling. It was just too much for her to process, shaking her head violently back and forth, hunching into herself she shuddered, and the cream-colored wolf burst out from her, ripping the clothes to shreds that rained down like confetti.

With her eyes on Lex Kayla missed the tears in Kian's eyes as he watched her. She ran out the still open front door, her nails clacking on the wood. The first breath of cold sharp air out of the house Kayla threw her head back and let out a mournful howl. Sending all her pain up into the sky so it wasn't locked inside of her anymore. Running to her home she saw Kole walk out of the house with a duffle bag in his clenched fist. He saw her coming and held his hand up with a sharp "no", and it stopped her in her tracks. He was always more dominant than she was; apparently, he was Second only to the Alpha. The look of shocked disgust on his face as she sat on her haunches unable to approach any closer broke her heart. "I'm so fucking sorry, I didn't know I could order you around Kay. Shit, I've got to go. I'm no good here right now," he said jumping into his truck and peeling out.

Chapter 10

The next morning after Kayla had exhausted the worst edge of her pain she shifted back, and took a shower. Remembering that she left her SUV over at Kian's house she walked over to pick it up. Her oldest brother was sitting on the front step, clearly waiting for her. Kian looked like he hadn't slept, and his eyes still utterly shattered. Kayla quickened her step as he stood up until she was running, and crashed into his arms. The siblings held onto each other like two survivors clinging to the only shred of hope left after a tragedy. Kian ran his hand up and down Kayla's back, offering the only comfort to be had. Nothing could be fixed, but he was letting her know that he was right there for her, where he always was. Determined not to cry again Kayla took a big breath to steady her emotions before pulling away.

"Kole's gone, Kian, and I don't know when he's coming back. He packed a bag last night," Kayla told him. "I'm so worried about him."

"Me too Kay. But he is a grown man, and if he needs time and space, then we have to respect that. Forcing him to come back will only succeed in pushing him away from us further," Kian said as much to her as to himself.

"There's more Kian. He was walking out with a bag when I came running up. He put his hand up and said 'no.' It stopped me in my tracks. He gave me an order, and I was compelled to obey him." Kayla was afraid of what that meant.

"A dominant Second can give a lower member an order Kay. Kole has a powerful wolf in him. We haven't gotten around to establishing rankings yet, I guess he just put his hat in the ring for Second, if he comes back." Kian ran his hand through his hair. The wind was picking up, and snow was starting to fall around them. "I was thinking oatmeal for breakfast this morning, with berries and sugar sprinkled on top like Mom always made us. Come on in."

With no other plans for the day, and feeling the need to be around her family Kayla followed

Kian inside for some breakfast. Some time after she had wolfed out last night Jase and Lex left for their homes too. The only people there were Kayla, Kian and Emma. They didn't say much as they ate the warm soothing oatmeal. Whether it was the nostalgia, or just having something warm in her belly Kayla was starting to feel marginally better. Learning the details of her father's death last night had reopened the wound, so anything that dulled that pain was alright with her.

Kayla helped clean the kitchen up after the simple meal. Kian told her that he would call their Mom and tell her everything. She wasn't thrilled with leaving that task up to Kian alone, but unfortunately she had to work at Dusty's today. They were decently busy for both lunch and dinner on weekends. Pulling into work she accepted that this restaurant didn't have a place in her life anymore. Somewhere in the middle of reorganizing the files at Decker Construction Kayla knew she didn't want to hire someone else and train them to replace her. Five years waiting tables and serving drinks here was enough. This place had paid her bills and kept her fed. It had also given her an escape from dealing with her baggage when she needed it. There just wasn't any time to think about your feelings when you're running around ragged all night. It was time for her to be a grown up, and grownups didn't hide from themselves, and maybe if she stepped aside someone else who needed everything this place had to offer would be able to take her place.

Walking in and heading straight for the office in the back she took a deep steadying breath and knocked on the door. Dusty, the owner, called her in. He was somewhere in his middle age, with wiry steel gray hair and a full beard. He had watered down brown eyes, that spoke to years of drinking too much. He used to drink at the bar every night like a regular. But he had gotten sober a few years ago. Now he was only there a few days a week, and spent his time predominantly in the office doing paperwork, or checking inventory in the stock room. Being a recovering alcoholic who owned a bar had to be one hell of a temptation, but he was making it work. "Oh, hey Kayla. How are you feeling? Carl told me you had some bad Chinese the other day."

"I'm OK now, thanks. I was actually wondering if you had time to talk before I went on shift?" Kayla smiled at him. He was decent, as far as bosses went, even if he was a bit absent the last few years.

"Uh, yeah. Actually, I was going to call, hoping to catch you before you left. I was doing the scheduling, and it took a bit longer than I planned. No matter, now is as good a time as any. Since you're working at the family business now, you know we had to hire a few new waitresses. I guess I took for granted just how much you handled here. What I'm trying to get at here is, maybe it's time you move on," Dusty said looking uncomfortable.

"Are you firing me?" Kayla asked on a disbelieving laugh.

"No! Not firing you like we don't want you anymore. Saying that I don't think you should be busting your hump trying to juggle two jobs unless you really need this. If you tell me straight up right now that you can't lose this job, then it's yours." Kayla shook her head slowly. "I didn't think so. You're a great girl Kayla, and I really like you. I don't want to let you go, but you don't owe this place anything."

"I was going to give you my two-week notice. I pulled in here today and I realized that this job wasn't right for me anymore, and that someone else should have it. I used to love my job here. It kept me busy, I got to chat people up, and the tips were good. Now it's just an obligation," she said with a sigh of relief.

"I thought so. Been around long enough to see when someone is changing and needs to move on along. You're free, girl, get on outta here. Unless you're wanting some lunch." Dusty smiled at her.

"No hard feelings?" Kayla asked. This place used to feel like a part of her, and she wasn't willing to leave it on a sour note.

"Absolutely not. You ever find yourself in need of a job again you let me know. But somehow I don't think you will." He handed her the paycheck she hadn't stopped in to get yesterday and Kayla walked back out.

Sitting in the car with the whole day open to her now she wasn't quite sure what to do with it. That hadn't gone anything like she expected it to. Not that she thought Dusty would give her a hard time, but she planned on doing the right thing, giving notice and working her two weeks. Her first impulse was to see what Lex was doing, and usually she would have stubbornly fought that, and headed home. But she was sick of fighting with herself. What good was it anyway. It only bought her misery in the end. Embracing the new freer Kayla she headed over to Lex's house.

He wasn't home when she got there, probably at work. Since it was barely lunch time, he must have had a day shift today. Still parked in Lex's driveway Kayla pulled her phone out of her purse and shot a text off to him.

So I'm free today, would you like to hang out tonight?

Setting her phone back in her still opened purse Kayla drove home. It dinged with a text just as she was unlocking her door.

Nope. I don't wanna hang out with you Kay. I wanna date you, make love to you, and then sleep next to you.

Holy hell that man could make her weak in the knees with a single text. Accepting that she might be a goner she couldn't help but smile as she replied.

So wanna come over and grill some steaks while I bake potatoes and mix a salad? There's a high likelihood of sex, and I might not kick you out afterward.

While waiting for Lex to reply Kayla walked around gathering up all the dirty clothes to wash. Laundry might not be very exciting, but nobody else was going to do it for her. Her phone dinged again.

Well how can I turn down that offer? I'll be there at six. Can't wait!

***

Kayla set some steaks out to thaw and washed, folded, and put away all the laundry. She caught up on episodes of her favorite show that were waiting on her DVR. It was a nice feeling looking forward to having a man over for dinner. Especially one who looked good enough to eat, made her laugh, and who enjoyed giving her multiple orgasms. That never hurt. Some men saw a woman's orgasm as just a means to an end. Kind of like, get her off so you can get off. Kayla had been with one or two men who thought like that. Why bother coming back for seconds when the first time didn't knock your socks off? It wasn't like that with Lex, he was different. He really enjoyed her body, and pleasing her made him feel good too. A man like Lex would never put his own needs ahead of her own. Her orgasm would never be just another step along the way, like checking off a list of things to do.

Kayla decided since this was a date, and their first official one, she really wanted to look the part, wow him. At five o'clock she walked upstairs to shower and shave. Stepping out she rubbed fragrant body cream all over her skin. Standing in front of her full body mirror Kayla tried on three separate outfits before landing on the deep aubergine wrap dress. Popping in some delicately beaded dangle earrings she walked back into the bathroom. Kayla spent some time perfecting her makeup. Smoking up her blue eyes a little more than usual and slicking on a nude gloss instead of her usual pink. Rubbing some pomade between her hands to warm it up she went to work making her short pixie cut look effortlessly sexy with just enough volume and sass. Checking the time, she walked back into her room slipping on strappy gunmetal colored heels. Kayla looked at herself one last time in the mirror. Deciding Lex wasn't going to know what hit him she smiled and walked down the steps just as she heard his truck pull into the drive.

Chapter 11

Waiting until Lex made it up the walk, but before he could knock on the door, Kayla opened it. As soon as she saw the look on his face she knew the effort was well worth it. He looked sucker punched, his face gone completely slack, one hand still raised, poised to knock. Finally recovering the use of his faculties after a beat he swept his eyes hungrily down her body and back up. With a knowing smile on her face Kayla took a step towards him leaned up and softly kissed him on the cheek. He had a bottle of wine held in his other hand, and she took it from him to walk into the kitchen leaving him to trail in her wake.

"The potatoes are almost ready, why don't you fire up the grill while I throw the salad together? I know it's snowing some, but the grill is on the side of the porch and protected from the elements," Kayla said turning her head to look at him as he walked into the kitchen a full minute after she did.

"Yeah, OK, I can do that. You look astonishing by the way. Absolutely stunning Kay," Lex said with a smile that lit up the whole room. He was dressed in a light blue button-down shirt with dark jeans that looked much newer than the ones he usually wore. He had scruff along his jaw, but it looked purposeful instead of lazy. Clearly, she wasn't the only one who thought to dress up for their date.

"Thank you, you don't look so bad yourself Kolter," Kayla teased. Adding a wink at the end so he didn't think she was using his last name as a barrier between them like she used to.

"I have one problem though," Lex said walking up next to her. "That cheek kiss wasn't enough for me. I need to taste you." Tipping her head up with a thumb under her chin he leaned down. The kiss simmered softly with passion. The desire was there, but with no rush to consume. Lex kissed her like a man who knew he had all night to savor and was planning on enjoying taking his time with her. Pulling away just before Kayla went weak in the knees, he grabbed the waiting steaks and sauntered out of the kitchen towards the back door and waiting grill. Kayla stood there in awe. He had never kissed her like that before. Their kisses had been blazing with heat, or that one soft and sweet in front of the pack. Touching the tips of her fingers to her lips to hold all the sensations in, Kayla reminded herself to breathe.

After chopping the vegetables for the salad Kayla pulled the potatoes out of the oven. She was just walking the food over to the table when Lex came in carrying the platter filled with steaks. "I forgot to ask, I hope you still like it medium rare," he said setting the plate down.

"I do, thank you." Kayla wasn't surprised that Lex knew her preferences, but it still made her feel all warm and fuzzy inside. Lex pulled her chair out from under the table for her to sit down. "Aren't you quite the gentleman?"

"Well, I am a great date, ask anyone." Lex grinned at her. "The rest is just good manners though. My Mom would expect no less."

Laughing at that remembering how hard both of their mothers had worked to instill some manners in them when they were cubs. "Well, I think its sexy. And who exactly should I direct my questions about your dating skills to?"

"See now if my Mom had told me that women would find manners sexy they would have stuck much quicker!" Lex laughed. "And I'm a man who knows better than to answer that question."

"Smart man, Lex. But I bet you would have fought them even harder back then, just so you never ended up catching some girl's cooties."

"You might actually be right on that one. I remember thinking it was gross how often my parents wanted to kiss each other," Lex said grabbing a second baked potato.

"Yeah, me too. I didn't think I would ever want some boy sticking his tongue in my mouth.

Turns out its pretty nice," Kayla said, her eyes laughing while munching on a bite of her salad.

"Just nice? Well then I need to up my game," Lex said with an arch of his eyebrow.

"You might. So how was your day?" she asked.

"Pretty boring actually, and trust me, I'm not complaining about that. I gave a couple of speeding tickets, there was one minor car accidents, no injuries, just some traded paint. What about you?" Lex said as he finished the last of his steak.

"Mine was a little unexpected actually. I kind of got let go from Dusty's, which freed my night up to spend with you." Kayla smiled at him. "Great job on the steaks too."

"Wait, you got fired? For what?" Lex looked shocked, edging towards annoyed.

"Not quite fired, exactly. But it's okay. I actually decided I was going to give my notice today, and when I went in to do it Dusty told me that he didn't think my place was there anymore. Some old bar logic about moving on I guess. I'm a little scared to be honest, I got a job there as soon as I was eighteen and old enough to be hired. I got eight years there. But my life lately is heading in a different direction, and that's a good thing. At least, I hope so." Kayla sipped the wine he brought.

"So you're really liking working in the office at Decker Construction then? Kian isn't being too big of a pain in your ass?"

"Yeah, I really like it. Kian will always be my bossy older brother, but now that he has a mate it's easier to deal with. It seems like I was meant to be there, I know that sounds kind of cliche. Kind of like it's part of taking the pack in a new direction. I found myself dreading going into work at the bar. So it was probably way past time for a change."

"There have been a lot of changes lately. It's hard to think that not too long ago your uncle was still the Alpha, and we had never met Emma," Lex said staring off absently.

"Yeah, it's kind of crazy to think about, but at the same time, it feels like Emma has always been here. She just fits, I guess, like a mate should. I always wondered what kind of mates my brothers would end up with, and if I would like them, or if they would feel like thieves stealing them away from me. I know fate shows our perfect mates, but that doesn't mean everyone else adjusts so smoothly," Kayla said standing up to clear away plates from the table.

"I was always afraid you would find someone else," Lex admitted quietly as he gathered up dishes to help.

"Me too. I was waiting for the day you would bring a mate around. I wasn't sure how I was going to be able to handle that." Kayla was rinsing the plates off and loading them into the dishwasher.

"We sure wasted a lot of time trying to stay away from each other and pretend there was nothing between us," Lex leaned back against the counter watching.

Kayla finished loading the dishwasher. "There is no denying this chemistry now. We burn so hot together I am surprised it didn't melt us." She walked up to Lex stopping just shy of touching him.

"Speak for yourself. I feel pretty scorched." Lex ran his hand up Kayla's arm and cupped the back of her neck. His thumb stroking gently just behind her ear.

Kayla stared up at him, her eyes endless pools of shimmering blue. Her lips no longer shimmering with gloss after the meal. Now they looked plump and she was biting the bottom one between her teeth. Watching her work those white teeth over that lip snapped the restraint Lex had been holding himself together with. Kayla could see the change from flirtatious to hungry in his eyes. His hunger immediately igniting her own. Grabbing the hand he had behind her head and lacing her fingers with his Kayla turned and led him up the stairs towards her room.

Lex didn't fight to lead, or say anything on the way up. He just followed her, along for the journey however she chose to play it. Damn but that man was sexy, and he didn't even know it. Letting her set the tone was slightly intoxicating. Once they were up inside Kayla's bedroom she gave him a nudge towards the foot of the bed. Getting the hint Lex sat down. Kayla's bedroom was large, a white four poster king sized bed with sunny yellow bedding dominated one wall, another wall had two large windows, the curtains left open leaving the room drenched in moonlight. The third wall had a large dresser with a television on top, the doors for the closet and attached bathroom, and the final wall was white bookshelves. Filled with books, small treasures, and pictures of her family. The walls were a refreshing spring green, and paired with the white furniture it was decidedly feminine, but without frills much like the woman herself.

Sitting at the foot of the bed, feet resting on the floor Lex stared into Kayla's eyes. She could smell the hormones rolling off him, his erection pressing against the seam of his pants. And yet he sat and waited for her next move. Powerful, dominant Lex, completely at ease to let her set the pace. Enjoying the slow simmering heat in her belly, Kayla reached up and slid the beaded earrings out, setting them atop the dresser. She ran her hands seductively down her own body, and Lex licked his lips. Kayla untied the front of her aubergine wrap dress opening it to show Lex the charcoal lace of her push up bra and matching thong. Her dusty pink nipples visible through the barely-there lace. His fingers gripped the comforter where they rested behind him. Turning around Kayla let the dress slide all the way off her body. Looking over her shoulder she saw hot silver starting to bleed into his beautiful brown eyes. The stark hunger in his eyes fanned the flames of her desire.

Reaching up Kayla unhooked the back of her bra with one hand, catching it with the other, and tossing it in his direction. Her head still turned back toward him she let her hands roam her body once more. Teasing Lex that he knew her hands were molding her breasts, but he couldn't see. It felt so good that she moaned before running her hands down to her hips. Hooking her thumbs in the sides of her already soaked panties she tugged them down. Bending at the waist Kayla leaned over never letting go of the thongs until she was stepping out of them.

Still bent over she ran her hands back up her legs. She was hot and wet already, and she stroked a finger over her clit. Lex let out a growl as he watched the finger dip inside of her.

Smiling to herself Kayla stood back up and sauntered over to her lover in nothing but the strappy gunmetal shoes. Walking into the space between his knees Lex's hands immediately came up to touch. Shaking her head and setting his hands back down Kayla began to unbutton his shirt slowly while rotating her hips in circles so that she was rubbing the inside of each of his thighs. Kayla opened his shirt sliding her hands in to push it off his shoulders. His skin was hot to the touch, as she ran her hands down his muscled pecks, down the chiseled abs. Unsnapping his jeans she ran the zipper over the length of him with a slow rip. Going down to her knees in front of him she pulled his boxers down enough to free his dick. It was completely hard already, veins straining, a bead of moisture at the tip. Licking her lips in anticipation Kayla slid her mouth down as far as she could.

Taking him in until he was filling the back of her throat.

Moaning at how good it felt to have him in her mouth Kayla pulled her head back, until his dick almost popped out, before going down again. Setting a devastatingly slow rhythm she worked his dick until they were both breathless. Kayla stepped back letting Lex stand up and out of the tangle of pants at his ankles. Setting her hands on his shoulders she finally leaned up and kissed him. Lex ran his hands down her sides, hooking the back of her legs and lifting her up and over his dick. Kayla was so wet he slipped easily in. Standing a foot away from the bed, and without pressing her back against anything. Lex held her hips in his hands and rocked his hips, his dick sliding in and out slowly.

Looking into his eyes Kayla held on to his shoulders and just absorbed how good this felt. Lex was so strong; no man had ever had her like this before. With each slow stroke his dick slid across her sensitive clit, Kayla's toes still in the heels were curling. The pressure was building deep inside, her body starting to tremble. Lex didn't pick up the pace even though Kayla was whimpering in desperation now, her body straining to race towards completion. Wrapping her arms tight around his shoulders, his rough chest hair tickling against the tips of her nipples. With a growl Kayla's pussy gripped his dick as the pulsing waves of orgasm slid over her.

Lex carried her over the bed and laid her down gently. Kayla was expecting him to lay down on top of her. Instead, he slid down and nibbled along her inner thigh. Sliding his finger inside where her aftershocks were still pulsing. "Ooooooooooooo," she said leaning up to watch him. He sucked and bit the inside of her thighs while working his finger in and out slowly. Kayla was frustratingly close again. "Please, faster, I'm almost there," she gasped out.

"You'll get there, baby, we've got all night," Lex said, his mouth pressed against her leg. "Unless you wanna help me. That little show was the sexiest fucking thing I've ever seen. Show me how you like to touch yourself."

Without any hesitation Kayla reached down pressing two fingers against her wet clit and rubbed in circles. Lex added a second finger to the one stroking inside of her. On a long drawn out "Yesssssss," Kayla came all over both of their hands.

Lex climbed up her body and slid inside her pussy before she could come down from the high of release. Pumping in deep and hard, but still so slow Lex leaned down and kissed her. He slid his tongue across hers in time to the rhythm of his hips. Kayla gripped his hair in her hands and kissed him back with everything she had. He felt so good, filling her up completely, their bodies making a slick sound as they met. Moaning loudly with every stroke in, Kayla was getting close again. She pressed her legs hard against Lex's hips. Lex growled and reached down between them holding her legs wide open. He finally quickened his punishingly slow pace and pumped into Kayla faster and faster. Kayla could feel his dick swelling impossibly bigger, and knew he was just as close as she was. Gripping his lip in between her teeth she shattered, her back bowing with the massive orgasm. Lex let out a loud growl and pressed his hips to hers, his dick twitching erratically inside of her, filling her with warmth.

They lay locked together like that for a while, their hearts racing. A satisfied smile on Kayla's face. Lex brushed the spikes of hair back from her face with his hand gently. "You're my mate, Kayla."

Chapter 12

Knowing that he couldn't take the words back now that he said them out loud Lex watched Kayla. He knew she flinched at what he said because he was still buried deep inside her body. There were a million different emotions racing past her eyes, too quickly for him to follow. Fear was there at the forefront, which he expected, but he saw happiness flit through too. "I wasn't planning on saying that." Lex lifted himself off Kayla and sat up. Running his hand through his hair. "Don't ask me to leave."

Kayla sat up and reached down unstrapping the shoes still on her feet. Lex had never had a woman with her shoes still on before. There was something so sexy about it, he didn't harbor some secret foot fetish, but she could leave them on every time from now on if she wanted. That was hot as hell.

"I don't want you to leave Lex. That doesn't surprise me, my wolf has been screaming that at me for a while now. I just wasn't expecting you to come out and say it like that," Kayla said.

Her skin was still covered in a sheen of sweat, and there were red marks from him on her thighs. He had scraped her neck up some with his beard too. Her skin was so delicate. Seeing evidence of him on her skin filled him with pride, and guilt in equal parts. Running a finger along the side of her neck he said, "My beard scraped you, maybe I should shave it all off."

"I like the bite of it. Leave it. I'll heal before morning." She rested her palm against the scruff on his cheek. "Being your mate scares me. That means letting you all the way in. It hurt so much losing you before, and I only had a single moment with you back then. It would rip me to shreds now Lex. I saw how losing my Dad hollowed out my Mom's soul." Her shaky words were barely loud enough to hear, even with shifter hearing.

"I'm scared too Kayla," Lex said taking her hand in his. "You could hurt me just as much as I could hurt you. I don't want to hurt you though. I want to make you happy, always. Maybe you should ask your Mom if the risk is worth the pain."

Pulling the covers down Kayla climbed into bed still holding Lex's hand in hers. "Nobody has ever held me while I slept before," she told him.

"Me either." Lex knew that there would be no more talk of mates tonight. They both had to let it sink in and adjust to the idea. Pulling Kayla's head on his chest he stroked her hair until long after she drifted off. Sleep didn't find Lex for a few hours, instead he lay there listening to her breathing slowly in and out. Lex knew without a doubt that there was no sound in this world more precious to him than that, and that he would do absolutely anything for Kayla. Even if she asked him to leave her alone. The happiness of the woman in his arms mattered more to him than his own.

***

Kayla stretching woke him up, and when he peeled his eyes open the sun was just starting to lighten the room. She was still warm with sleep and pressed up against him. Her eyes still hazy and unfocused. Leaning up he pressed his lips to hers. The soft sound in the back of her throat was all the encouragement he needed. Lex rolled her over and buried his dick deep within her. "You're always wet for me Kay," he gasped easing out of her slowly and pushing back in, setting a lazy rhythm.

"You feel so good, I can't get enough," Kayla said pulling his face in for a kiss. As soon as his lips touched hers she was pushing her tongue into his mouth. Rubbing it against his, making little whimpering noises with every pump of his dick.

Needing more, Lex went up on his knees and pumped into her faster. Kayla's hips rose up, eagerly meeting his beat for beat. Lex grabbed her legs with each arm and pushed them up over his shoulders. The new angle had him sliding deeper inside and brought a growl bubbling up from her throat. "Oh my god Lex, yes, yes, yes!" she punctuated with each breath.

"So deep, I'm close Kay, come with me!" His balls were slapping against her ass as he pistoned in and out of her wet heat. He held her hips down with one hand, his thumb reaching over to press against her clit. Kayla's legs were starting to shake, so Lex knew she was getting close. Gritting his teeth, trying to hold it together he rocked his hips faster and faster, harder and harder. With the first clench of her pussy grabbing his dick her eyes flew open, burning silver. Watching her shatter around him Lex let it go, pumping his release into Kayla on a loud growl.

She felt so good surrounding him, he couldn't stop rocking in and out of her until he absorbed every one of her aftershocks. Kayla was breathing hard, her cheeks pink, and a smile glowing on her face. "Damn Lex. You're officially invited to stay over as often as you want to if you wake up this horny every morning," she laughed out.

"This is just a natural response to waking up to a beautiful woman pressed against me." She smelled like him, and satisfaction. Knowing they were bonding together because he could feel her happiness streaking through him he licked along her jaw.

"Lex, it's not going down," Kayla gasped out as his tongue snaked up to her ear. She rocked her hips against his.

"Perks of being a shifter. That, and you're the sexiest woman I've ever seen. There will never come a day when I don't want you." He gave her what she wanted and pulled out of her slowly before surging back in.

Kayla grabbed his hips, dragging him against her, the nails on her fingers digging into the skin on his ass urging him on. Lex leaned down pulling one of her nipples into his mouth sucking hard. She cried out. Encouraged by the sound he bit down rolling the bud between his teeth. Kayla arched her back, and he snaked his arm underneath pulling her into his chest, pumping into her harder and harder. Kayla was kissing up the front of his neck. He was dragging air in and out, panting. Pushing them both towards the edge of the cliff. At the first pulsing wave of her orgasm, he felt her teeth sink deep into his skin. Right where his neck met his shoulder. Completely lost to sensations now Lex cradled her head encouraging her teeth deeper as he growled and emptied himself into her again in erratic spurts.

"Oh my God, Lex. I'm so sorry, I claimed you. I didn't want to, I didn't mean to. It just happened," Kayla gasped. His blood smeared all over her lips.

"You gotta finish it. Say it, or it won't count," he said looking down at her.

"I can't. I'm sorry, I'm not ready for this. My wolf pushed me into biting you, I'm not ready damn it," Kayla pushed him off her and ran across the room to the bathroom. Lex heard the click of the lock before the shower started. Thinking she needed space right now, he pulled on his clothes and walked out.

Thinking that wasn't exactly how he planned on spending his morning he drove home. Looking down at the blood all over his neck and chest Lex figured a shower needed to happen first, so he didn't freak anyone out. He knew the wound was already closing thanks to his shifter healing, but that didn't magically make the blood he had shed disappear. Tossing his shirt in the trash as he walked past towards the bathroom. There was no way all that blood would ever wash out. Taking a look at the damage in the mirror.

He wanted to be claimed by Kayla. That was the next step after finding your mate. But getting bitten and then being pushed away wasn't how it was supposed to happen. This was supposed to be a happy monumental moment, and right now it just felt like a letdown. Like Christmas morning, opening the biggest, prettiest present and finding out there was nothing inside. His wolf was howling in desperation inside of him. Trying to convince him to go back to Kayla, but it would do no good. Lex was struggling with patience and understanding and feeling more heartbroken than he wanted to admit. "WHY AM I NOT GOOD ENOUGH?" Lex shouted into the mirror at his reflection. Unable to stand looking at himself anymore he turned around and sank down onto the tiled floor, his head in his hands.

Chapter 13

Scrubbing furiously at her skin, trying to wash all of Lex's blood off, Kayla was in full-fledged freak out mode. How in the hell could she have done that to him? All shifters grew up hoping to find their mate, and the number one rule was not to claim someone unless they wanted it. That had linked him to her now. She was feeling so mad at her damn wolf for pushing her into biting Lex. There was a pretty happy wolf inside of Kayla right now though. *He is our mate, he wanted to claim us, you think too much. Go to him.* Shaking her head and refusing to answer the wolf she turned her face into the water. The metallic taste of his blood was still clinging to her tongue, so she opened her mouth letting it fill up with the warm water. Swishing it around and spitting it out didn't seem to erase all traces of it. She felt like a monster for the first time in her life. She was selfish and had taken the choice away from him. Just like her Uncle took what he wanted from people. So disgusted with herself that hot bile rushed up her throat, and had Kayla stumbling out of the shower towards the toilet, barely able to make it in time. There wasn't much in her stomach to empty, but that didn't stop her from heaving repeatedly.

Resting her head on her arm across the toilet the first tears streaming down her face. Last night with Lex was almost perfect, this morning was amazing, and then she had gone and ruined everything. How could Lex be with her now? She bit him, but panicked and didn't say the claiming words. Swiping the tears off her face with the back of her hands, she stood up and stepped back into the still running shower to clean up. Washing her hair, and body quickly Kayla turned off the taps and grabbed a towel.

Walking back into her room Lex was gone. Taking a deep breath that she didn't have to face him just yet she pulled on some yoga pants and a simple bright red t-shirt. It was a little too baggy on her so she gathered it at the small of her back in a little knot. Running her fingers through her hair she looked over at the bed. The whole room smelled like sex, both of their scents mingling together. There were only a couple of blood drops on the sheets. But those little red splatters reminded her just how badly she had messed up. Grabbing all the bedding she frantically ripped it off the mattress. Running it down the stairs she shoved as much as she could into the washing machine. Pouring laundry detergent over it she noticed just how badly her hands were shaking. A quiet desperation flooded through her, which made no sense because Kayla was feeling disgusted with herself, and furious, but not desperate. It was Lex! Biting had linked them together, and she was picking up on his emotions. Which only made her feel even worse about what she had done.

Kayla was still standing in front of the washing machine when Emma walked into the house calling her name. "Hey Kayla, wanna go shopping with me today? I could use some girl time."

"I'm in here," Kayla said from the laundry room.

When Emma walked in the smile on her face dropped. "What's the matter Kay? You're shaking like a leaf, and are those tear streaks on your face?" Emma wrapped her arms around Kayla and rocked them gently back and forth.

"I messed everything up Em, I'm just as selfish as Russ! I messed up, and I lost Lex forever," Kayla sobbed into Emma's shoulder.

"Okay, it's okay, we can fix whatever it is. You're not Russell, don't you ever think that! Lex loves you. We can fix this." Emma rubbed her hands up and down Kayla's back. "Tell me what happened."

"I invited him over to dinner last night, for our first date. He brought wine, grilled the steaks, I baked potatoes and made a salad. It was the best date ever. Then we went upstairs and had knock your socks off sex. He told me I was his mate. And it was actually a relief hearing him say it out loud. My wolf has been screaming it at me, but hearing him was different, felt like more ya know. I let him sleep over, which is huge for me, and this morning we did it again, twice. It was so intense, and my wolf kept telling me it was time, to claim him as my mate, and I tried to fight it, but she kept pushing, and pushing. I bit him, without asking Emma. I didn't ask him. I took what I wanted without permission. I'm a fucking monster like my Uncle!" Kayla said still clinging to Emma.

"You say that again and I'm gonna get really pissed Kayla. You are not your uncle! One mistake doesn't make you a monster. Let me get this straight. You two had an awesome date, followed up by even better sex, and he told you that you're his mate. You let him sleep over even after he said that? But this morning completely caught up in the moment you claimed him? What did he say? Was he upset about it?" Emma asked.

"He asked me to finish it and say the claiming words. I just couldn't and I ran into the bathroom," Kayla answered finally backing out of Emma's arms enough to look in her face.

"You didn't finish it? Oh no, Kayla, that can't be good. Where is Lex now? I didn't see the cruiser or his truck out front." Emma walked into the kitchen. Settling Kayla on a stool she started some coffee.

"He was gone when I got out of the shower. Which is a good thing I guess because he didn't hear me upchucking, and I didn't have to face him." Kayla rested her head in her hands.

"You threw up?" Emma asked.

"I could still taste his blood, and I was disgusted with myself. I can feel him now, Em, I chained him to me," Kayla said, her voice tapering off a whisper at the end.

"Oh, baby, it will be okay. He loves you. He wanted you to complete the claiming ritual. Once he claims you then the link will go both ways," Emma assured her. "Sex between mates is always very intense, but it gets even more so once the bond starts happening. That's probably what happened. You started opening your heart to him, and the bond that had been years in the making kind of rushed to life."

"It gets more intense? Every time we touch it's like we are starving for each other," Kayla said doubtfully.

"Yeah. Think of it like this, right now you're only feeling your own pleasure but pretty soon you will be able to feel how good you make him feel too. It's so special, and exciting, and it will never be boring like it would with another." Emma set warm steaming mugs of coffee in front of Kayla and settled on the stool beside her.

"Like when I touch him I will feel it?" Kayla asked.

"Not quite. But you will feel that he is overwhelmed with sensations, that he is so happy, turned on, and how deep his love goes. Feeling that enhances the physicality of it. It's like making love body and soul," Emma explained.

"Why would he want to be with me after I took his choice away though? How am I ever going to be able to fix that?" Kayla said dejectedly.

"It got intense, I'm positive that he will understand. You pushing him away again is probably the bigger problem. You wanted him enough to claim him, but not enough to follow through. Kayla, you're so upset that you didn't ask to claim him, but do you realize that he is probably feeling like you didn't want him? Maybe regretted biting him?" Emma shook her head sadly.

"Shit. You're right. I got so caught up in my own head, that I didn't think about how I pushed him away again. I've gotta go fix it." Kayla stood up and went to put shoes on. "I'm sorry I can't go shopping with you today."

"That's okay, I will just drag Kian along," Emma said as Kayla was walking out the door. "Go on and get your man."

Chapter 14

Kayla's car screeched to a stop in Lex's driveway. Putting it in park she rushed to the door. Banging on it she called out, "Lex, I'm so sorry, I need to make this right." Trying the knob, she found it was locked. "Lex! Please let me talk to you!" she shouted. Kayla was turning away from the door to head to the back and knock there when he answered.

"Why are you here Kayla? You don't want me as your mate." Lex looked miserable. He was in faded jeans and a white t-shirt with no socks on his feet. "Just go away."

Before she could say anything, he shut the door in her face, and there was a distinct clicking of the lock. Stunned, Kayla just stood there. He told her to go away. She came here to try and make it right, and he wasn't going to let her. Feeling ready to burst into tears or punch someone she walked back to her car and drove back home. Emma was still sitting in her kitchen when Kayla walked back in.

"Back so soon?" Emma asked her.

"Ugh, yeah, well it turns out Lex isn't interested in anything I have to say." Kayla paced back and forth in front of the counter. "I can't fix it if his stupid stubborn ass won't give me a chance to."

Emma picked up her phone, "I'll let Kian know that I'm gonna stay here today instead of shopping."

"I'm not really great company right now," Kayla said.

"I'm not expecting you to entertain me, but I can stay and be supportive. That's what best friends do," Emma said like she was stating the obvious.

"I'm your best friend?" Kayla asked a little shocked.

"Well duh." Emma tossed her auburn curls over her shoulder and arched an eyebrow at Kayla. "No getting out of it now."

Hugging Emma, Kayla shook her head. "It's nice to have a best friend."

Kian and Jase burst into the house as the two women were hugging. "Jase just rushed over to tell me that as he was leaving this morning, he smelled Russ outside his house. He's back." Kian walked right to Emma.

Turning immediately and walking out the back-door Kayla took a big sniff of the air. Shaking her head, she ran a circle around the house coming back in through the front. "I don't smell him here."

"He wasn't near my place either. Maybe he thought that it would be easier to get near Jase since he didn't see him every single day like I did. That he wouldn't notice," Kian answered. "Where's Lex?"

"At his place," Emma said looking over at Kayla. Friends didn't spill secrets. Kayla looked relieved that Emma didn't say more.

Kian pulled out his phone and called Lex. "My Uncle's back. He was hanging around Jase's house. Any sign at your place?" Kian paused to listen to Lex's answer. "Yeah, okay check it out and then come over here," Kian said and hung up.

"I'm going to let Kole know," Kayla said, calling her brother. Kole didn't pick up so Kayla left a message. "Kole, our uncle's back. Clearly planning something. Just be safe."

Kian's jaw was clenched so tight that it looked like it was about to break. He was filling the air with enough dominance and power that the hairs on Kayla's arms were standing up.

"I don't like this, don't like it at all. It feels off. Why would he come back now that nobody here supports him?" Jase asked the room.

"If he was keeping tabs on us maybe he knows that Kole left? Our pack is a man down, he never thought much of Lex, he probably thinks that it's a good time to strike," Emma said. "He is in for more of a fight than he realizes."

"Hell yeah he is! Nobody messes with my family, my pack like he has. Even without Kole that's still five against one. I like those odds," Kayla said.

Lex walked in the house then. "I don't smell Russell, but there was a shifter I don't recognize around my place. I think your uncle brought some back up."

Kian let out a ear splitting pissed off growl and walked out of the house. Taking off his clothes slowly and meticulously he turned and looked back at the rest of the pack with glowing silver eyes full of menace, before hunching his shoulders in and letting the wolf have him. One by one everyone stripped setting all their clothes into the pile with Kian's. Five wolves stood in the yard at the ready now. Their Alpha tipped his head back and howled, sending a clear warning into the air. Whoever was coming for Big Woods Pack was in for a fight.

Their paws crunched on the snow as they fanned out on either side of Kian before joining him in the howl. The sound of a phone buzzing in someone's pocket up on the porch was the only noise. Kayla hoped it was Kole letting them know he was safe. Unable to answer it in this form she shook her head and focused on the forest around them. These were her woods. She knew them like the back of her hand, and they wouldn't hide her uncle for long. Emma pressed her shoulder against Kayla's fur, clearly showing support. Kayla was grateful once again that Emma had a wolf now too. They were going to need all the snapping jaws they could get.

Another howl split the air deep within the woods. Recognizing it instantly as their former Alpha the pack took off at a thundering pace in the direction of the sound. Paws were crunching rapidly through the snow still deep in the shadowed woods. Jase was right, this was all off. Kayla didn't hear anyone running towards them to meet in battle like she should. Kian must have thought the same thing because he slowed the pack to a stop in front of them. Head up he sniffed the air, then shaking his head sneezed. Kayla smelled it then, bitterness, burning her nose. Sneezing once, twice trying to clear it from her nose. An engine rumbled to life a short distance away. Turning towards it Kayla took off at a sprint. There was a small access road, a two track through the woods that rangers with the Department of Natural Resources used.

An older model crew cab truck was speeding away when Kayla came to the road. Pushing herself until her muscles screamed Kayla chased after the truck. No license plate to memorize, but there were three men inside. The back driver's side window rolled jerkily down, manual windows Kayla noted. There was a loud cracking sound, and Kayla felt something rip through her chest. Kayla stumbled to a stop unable to chase the truck anymore. The man in the back that had shot her turned around, his face visible through the back window. Her uncle smiled and waved back at her the gun still in his hand.

Warmth was oozing down her fur. Struggling to stay upright Kayla finally realized that her bastard uncle has shot her. Thinking when she got her hands on him she was going to tear him limb from limb. She was the fastest runner in her pack and had pushed herself harder than ever. She could hear the others approaching now. The pain was radiating throughout her body, her legs beginning to go numb. Kian was the first to burst through the trees coming to a stop next to her. Kayla let out a yelp and gave in to the darkness pulling at her.

Chapter 15

The pack was running after Kayla, following her trail through the trees. She was so quick though; they were way behind her. Lex heard the shot ring out through the trees. He knew Kayla was down, just knew it. Kian was the first through the trees with Lex the barest breath behind. The beautiful cream wolf was dragging ragged gasps of air in and out, blood matting her chest. She let out a soft yelp and went limp. Panic flooded Lex and he nudged Kayla's head. She didn't respond. Emma and Jase made it to the road then. Standing over her Lex growled at the others. His mate was hurt. He wasn't there to protect her, and his mate was bleeding all over the road.

Kian was pacing nervously back and forth in front of him. Lex knew he needed to let them help Kayla, but he couldn't seem to make himself move away from her. With a grunt Emma folded her wolf away. Holding both hands up she said, "Let me help her Lex. I need to see the damage. Oh god, please Lex, I don't want to lose her either. Kayla is my best friend."

Lex knew she was right, his wolf's instinct to protect wasn't helping Kayla. With a monumental effort he took a step back. The second Kayla was clear of him Emma was on her. Feeling around for the source of the bleeding. "The bullet entered the upper right side of her chest." Running her hands across Kayla's shoulders. "Exit wound back here. Bullet isn't in her anymore, good, good. It broke the bone on the way out though." Standing up she looked right into Lex's eyes and said, "She'll be okay, she is already working to heal the damage. We have to carry her back though."

With a low rumbling growl Lex pushed the wolf down and shifted. Kneeling he scooped the woman he loved up and into his arms. Being careful not to jostle her too much he jogged back through the woods. Kian's dark golden wolf took point running in front of them, Emma back as a wolf was right by his side, and Jase followed behind bringing up the rear. It had only taken a few minutes running through the forest after Russell, but it took twenty of the longest minutes of Lex's entire life to get back. Kayla was passed out, but Lex could feel her through the bond. The pain she felt was staggeringly intense. His mate was a tough woman, but he was glad she wasn't lucid right now.

Kian shifted back blindingly fast as he was walking up the back steps. He was coming into his full Alpha power if he could shift back so easily on the fly like that. Lex walked into the door Kian held open, and not sure where else to put her Lex sat Kayla down on the kitchen table. Running his hands lightly across the soft fur of her muzzle he whispered reassurances. "My Kayla, you're back home now, it's going to be okay. You did good baby, real good. Emma said the bullet is out. We are all here, don't hurry back though, it's going to hurt, baby. Take your time. I've got you my love. I'm not going anywhere, and I've got you."

Emma checked her again, "The wounds are closing, but her shoulder is shattered. Anything I could do to help fix it she would just have to undo in the process of healing. She is healing though, and that's good. But it will take some time for that bone to knit itself back together." Kayla convulsed, shudders rippling over her slowly. "She is trying to change back. No, no! Kian, help her," Emma said.

"How can I help?" Kian said next to Emma. His blazing silver eyes were filled with worry.

"Order her to stay wolf for a little while longer. If she shifts back right now it could permanently disfigure her shoulder. Then she would lose the ability to use it. It needs a chance to fuse back together. She has to stay a wolf!" Emma said in a rush.

"Kayla, I need you to stay a wolf until I give you permission to shift back. Rest now, your body is working to fix itself," Kian said, his voice echoing with power.

Even in this condition Kayla wanted to obey the command of her Alpha. Her movements stilled for a moment then she started twitching again. "Jase, get me a bowl of warm water and a cloth. I want to clean some of this blood off, to get a better look at the wounds.," Emma said. Jase hurried into the kitchen to get what Emma asked for. "Lex, you need to try and calm down. I can feel the turbulence of your emotions, and I'm not linked to you like Kayla is. You're calling to her, and she will keep fighting to get back to you instead of to heal."

Looking over he saw Kian nod his head. Lex closed his eyes and concentrated on his breathing. Breath in, hold, let it out. He could do this for Kayla, he had to. His mate needed him to. Pulling from his experience of years wearing the uniform Lex settled himself, focusing on each muscle group at a time. Doing his very best to radiate calm strength for his Kayla, Lex opened his eyes back up. Jase walked back in with a large bowl of water and a handful of wash cloths.

"Okay, Kian, Jase, go get dressed, and bring our clothes inside too. I'm going to clean her up," Emma told them. "It's okay, go on," she added when both men stood there staring at her. Jase walked out first, then Kian. "I'm going to be as gentle as I can

Lex, seeing her like this hurts me too. I need to know that if she stirs in pain you aren't going to come at me," Emma said.

Looking into his cousin Emma's eyes Lex saw himself reflected. There was a desperate craziness on his face, his silver eyes almost feral. "I know you love her too Emma. I'm holding it together the best I can."

Nodding her head, "Well, that's enough for me then. Besides, if you hurt me she will tear you a new one," Emma said.

"Yeah, she will," Lex said as he watched Emma gently swipe the damp cloth across his mate's fur. Kayla didn't stir, and both he and Emma let out a relieved breath. She worked efficiently wiping up the blood, dunking the cloth into the bowl, ringing it out, before wiping again. When Kayla's fur went from red with blood to softly pink Lex could see the wound. It was closed now, thankfully. But it was large. Whoever shot her was using at least a 9mm, or a .45. That shot would have been catastrophic for a human, even without hitting anything vital the massive amount of blood loss would have been enough to kill. "He was trying to kill her."

"I know. A few inches over and it would have hit her spine, and he would have. She was running after the truck, so Russell's aim wasn't as accurate, thank god. But it was definitely not a warning shot," Emma replied. "That man has already taken too much from all of us."

Kian and Jase came in dressed with their arms full of clothes. Emma handed the bowl and cloth over to Lex. "Be very gentle with the exit wound, and remember it's going to look much worse than the entrance."

Nodding his head at her Lex knew she was right. But the first sight of the gaping hole was almost enough to buckle his knees. The wound was almost as big as his fist, and although it was closed now, it was red and raw. It would take weeks to fade into a scar that would mark her body forever. Swallowing the bile back that threatened to come up Lex carefully wiped as much blood away as he could. As a cop he had seen gunshot wounds before, but there was no way to prepare yourself when it was someone you loved. By the time Emma came back to the table with her clothes on a sheen of sweat had broken out all over his skin.

Taking the cloth from him Emma laid her hand on his arm. "You don't want to scare her when she comes to, Lex. Take a minute." Knowing she was right he went to grab his clothes from Kian.

"I'm sorry for growling at you Deck. I was doing it before I realized I was. Seeing her hurt and bloody like that made me pretty crazy I guess. She is my mate, but she is also your baby sister," he said pulling on his jeans.

"I know Lex. It was instinct to protect your mate. I don't blame you. I'm going to kill that fucking rat bastard for this." Kian ran his hand over his blonde beard, taking a deep breath he continued, "Just before we left someone's phone went off. It had to be yours or Kay's we already checked ours," Kian said.

Pulling his phone out of his pocket he shook his head, there were no missed calls or notifications.

Rummaging through the pile of Kayla's clothes he picked her phone up. She had a missed call and voicemail from Kole. Pressing play on the voicemail he turned it on speaker.

"Kay, what do you mean Russ is back? I'm a few hours away, but I'm heading back now. Shit, shit, shit! I never should have left. Call me back," Kole's recorded voice said.

Kian held his hand out for the phone. Lex handed it over. Kian dialed as they walked back over to the table by Kayla. Emma had one hand resting on Kayla's side feeling her breathing. Jase was standing in the corner his face a mask of anger, but the smell of worry wafted from his skin. Lex took a chair next to Emma, crossing his arms on the table and laying his head down by Kayla's.

Kole picked up on the third ring, the panic in his voice clear. "Kayla, fuck! It's been almost two hours. What's going on?"

"Kole, its Kian. Kayla is hurt bad." A loud growl was heard on the other end. "Let me get this out. We changed right after she called you. Russell was in the woods waiting. He howled giving away his location. Kayla took off after him, before I could tell her it was probably a trap, you know she has always been the fastest. He had a truck waiting and shot her as it pulled away. She took the hit in the chest, and it shattered her shoulder blade on the way out. She passed out just as we got to her so Lex carried her back here, and Emma has been taking care of her. She was all alone man."

"Shit Kian, shit! He shot her? He fucking shot Kayla?" Kole growled into the phone.

"Yeah, it looks like he was aiming to kill. She was chasing after the truck though, so she was harder to get a bead on. Emma said the bullet just barely missed her spine." Kian said.

"Let me talk to her."

"She is still unconscious Kole."

"Is she healing? She hasn't shifted back yet?"

"Emma said that if she shifts back before the bone knits itself back together, she will probably lose the full usage of it. The entrance and exit wounds have closed though, so the bleeding stopped. I told her to stay a wolf until I give her permission to change back."

"I am on my way; I will be there as soon as I can. But Kian, don't let your guard down. Russ knows you're all preoccupied right now, not to mention down two members. Stay alert. I will be there as soon as I can," Kole said.

"I know brother, I know. See you soon." Kian hung the phone up. "Kole is right, Russell could ambush us at any moment. Jase, you keep look out by the front, I will watch the back. We can't leave Kayla in here unprotected though because I don't put it past my uncle to come and try to finish her off."

Lex let out a warning growl. "Let him try."

Chapter 16

The pain radiating through Kayla as her body worked to heal itself was even worse than the actual bullet had been. That had felt shockingly quick and jarring as it ripped through her body. Healing felt like a million fires burning all throughout her body though. Knowing there was a lot of damage to heal had Kayla focusing on not fighting against the pain. She knew that everyone thought she was still unconscious, but she kept resurfacing for a few moments at a time. She smelled Lex next to her, felt Emma's hand on her side. Her pack needed her; they didn't know that there were people working with her uncle. But until she was healed enough to shift back, she couldn't tell them, no matter how much she wanted to. Her Alpha had ordered her to stay locked in wolf form when she tried to shift back earlier. She fought it trying to get the information to them, but her loyalty to her brother was all encompassing, and she had to obey.

The air was heavy with the scent of her own blood. Hours passed while she focused all her energy on simply breathing in and out, while the white-hot pain worked to heal her. It helped that Emma and Lex never left her side. She drifted away again, and their soft conversations, assuring each other that she was going to be okay, would bring her back up to the surface. Like an anchor to hold onto, helping her to stay conscious. The pain was cooling down to a throbbing ache when Kayla finally managed to open her eyes.

"Look! Her eyes are open," Lex said. "Kayla, thank god. You're okay. Let Emma check your shoulder. Don't move, baby."

Kayla felt Emma's hands running over the injured shoulder, assessing the progress. "The bone feels like it's back together, but it's going to hurt when she shifts," Emma said.

Looking into Lex's eyes she pleaded with him to understand. He stroked the fur on her muzzle. "I think she needs to shift back, Emma. Kayla is strong enough to handle the pain," Lex said.

"I know, I just wish I could take the pain from her, but if I give her anything it will just make her feel foggy. I'll go get Kian to release the order." Emma hurried away.

"Kayla, baby, I'm right here, and I'm not going anywhere, ever again," Lex told her. He shook his head as tears started to fill his eyes.

Emma rushed back in with Kian before Lex could say more. "Hey there little sister. Gave us quite a scare." Her brother couldn't hide the shaky relief in his voice. "As your Alpha I lift the order to stay wolf. You are free to shift back now, Kay." Kian filled the words with his power.

Growling with the effort, she gathered all of the strength she had within her, and Kayla worked to push the wolf down. Shifting always came with a measure of pain, one body didn't just mold and reshape into another without a cost. It was something all shifters learned to embrace, but this time the pain was searing. Not wanting to hurt her pack members Kayla gritted her teeth against the urge to cry out. It had been hard enough on everyone seeing her down and out with the injury. As soon as she was back in her skin Lex pulled her into a hug, doing his best to be gentle. Holding onto him Kayla took a deep breath, locking the pain down, and said, "Russell has help. There were two other men in the truck with him. I couldn't tell you before." Her voice was hoarse from lack of use.

"That makes sense. He must have recruited some rogues. They would be expendable to him, cannon fodder really. So he could use them for whatever he needed. That's why you kept trying to shift back isn't it? To warn us?" Kian asked.

"Part of the reason yes," she said looking at her brother. Turning to look at Lex she said, "I wanted to tell you I was going to be okay, Lex. You felt so scared, that it hurt me."

Holding her face in his hands Lex stared into her eyes. "I love you so much Kay, you're it for me. My mate, and I can't lose you. I'm sorry we wasted so many years." She nodded her head and pressed her face into his chest over his heart.

Remembering the call she made before, "Kole! I tried to get a hold of him before we shifted, is he okay?" Kayla said worriedly pulling away from Lex's embrace.

"I talked to him. He is rushing back right now, but he was some distance away. He is coming home Kayla," Kian said to her. "Our brother is coming home."

"I need a moment alone with Kayla," Emma said picking up Kayla's clothes and pulling her into the bathroom. Emma checked out the wound on her back, pressing on it, making sure the change didn't cause any additional harm. "Be honest with me. How bad is the pain? Don't you lie either," Emma asked.

"Not as bad as it was. Getting shot hurt, but healing was a real bitch. I've never been in so much pain before. I kept coming to, but the pain was so intense I couldn't even open my eyes. My chest aches, and there is a constant throbbing in my shoulder. But I can handle it. That asshole is not going to beat me," Kayla said with absolute conviction. Satisfied with the answer Emma handed over the red shirt and yoga pants Kayla had on earlier, and she pulled them on as gently as she could. "It's going to scar bad isn't it?" Kayla asked, allowing herself to be a little bit vain with the other woman.

"Yeah, it is. There isn't much I can do to fix that. But don't you dare be ashamed of your scars. These are literally signs that you were stronger than what came for you. You are one bad ass woman Kayla," Emma told her.

"Thanks, Em." Kayla hugged her. "For everything."

Chapter 17

"Kayla! Kayla!" she heard Kole shout as he ran into the house. Opening the bathroom door she could see the panic etched across her brother's face, his eyes blazing silver. He spotted her and ignoring everyone else inside the house he barreled toward her. Lifting her up in an embrace he chanted, "I'm sorry, I wasn't here Kay, god, I'm so sorry. I left and you got shot! Shit sis, I was so scared I was going to make it back here and all of you would be gone." He ran shaking hands over her shoulders, up and down her back. Needing to feel she was still in one piece. Seeing her hurt so bad had been hard on everyone there, but imagining the worst as he raced home was clearly hell on Kole.

"It's not your fault Kole. I'm stronger than a bullet, Russell can't put me down that easily," Kayla said meaning every word. "But I am glad you're back,

I really missed you." Having Kole back felt like all the pieces stitching themselves back together again.

"We all missed you brother." Kian walked over slinging an arm around each of his siblings. "Are you still Big Woods Pack, Kole, or are you a rogue helping us out this once?" Everyone stilling waiting for the answer.

"When I left, I was planning on coming back, I just needed to catch my breath. But then the further away I got the more I wondered if I was coming back. When Kayla called me, everything got really fucking clear then. This is my home. You guys are my pack, and I am done with running. Let's hunt that bastard down." A menacing grin broke across Kole's face, and Kayla knew that he wasn't the same man that had driven away a few nights ago.

"First we need to settle who is officially my Second. An Alpha is nothing without a strong Second at his back. Kayla told me you gave her an order Kole, and she was compelled to obey," Kian said.

"Yeah, I had no fucking idea I could do that. Guess we need to do this the right way." Putting his hand on his chest he continued. "Kole Decker, challenging for the rank of Second in the pack."

Kayla was the first to respond, "I have no challenge, since you can order me and all, I clearly don't out rank you."

Emma took a step back. "Mate to the Alpha is the only rank I want, I have no challenge."

"Well shit. If I don't, I will never know. Alexander Kolter, challenging for the rank of Second in the pack." Lex placed his hand on his chest.

"Nope, I'll leave that to the two of you. I have no challenge," Jase said from where he stood.

"As wolves, outside. Only until one of you establishes dominance," Kian said walking out the door.

Everyone followed along behind their Alpha. Kian waited until both men had stripped down and turned into the other half of themselves. The dark gray wolf with silver chest stood facing off against the dark brown wolf with the tan muzzle. Both awaiting orders from their Alpha they stood still.

"You will do this with respect, and honor for each other, or I will not accept the victor as my Second. Understood?" Kian waited until both giant animals dipped their heads in response. Taking a step back Kian folded his arms across his massive chest to watch the fight.

Respecting her mate's right to challenge for Second Kayla stood next to Emma and watched as her brother and lover circled each other slowly. Violence was integral to their way of life, and Kayla had watched her oldest brother's challenges to hold Second in the pack for years. It was clear watching the wolves that they took no pleasure in the pain they would inflict on each other in their path to establish which one of them was more dominant. The dark gray wolf was the first to make a move, lunging at his competitor. The deep brown wolf sidestepped dodging the teeth. The air was ripe with the snapping of teeth, and grunts of effort as they looped around each other trying to get at the others throat. The brown latched his teeth into the gray's shoulder biting down. Not ready to give up the gray growled and ripped himself out, his blood coloring the teeth of his foe. In a move so powerfully swift, before the brown wolf could react, the gray had his teeth firmly around his neck. Letting his body go still the brown wolf accepted the results. Kole released his grip on Lex's neck and Lex lowered himself closer to the ground bowing with respect to his new Second.

"Kole Decker, Second to the Alpha of the Big Woods Pack!" Kian yelled.

Both men shook out their fur and shifted back into men. Kole's shoulder was bleeding from the bite, as he held his hand out to Lex. "Good fight. You almost had it, man."

Accepting the offered shake Lex replied, "I would have too, but you have changed Kole. Grown into your dominance. I am proud to call you Second, man."

Kayla gave her congratulations with a traditional down turned head saying "My Second."

Emma, and Jase followed her lead addressing Kole the same.

"As Second I pledge my loyalty to you Kian, and to the Big Woods pack." Kole bowed his head ever so slightly to Kian.

"Now that's over, put your dicks away, and I say we go on the offense. Scope out where that rat bastard is hiding, so he doesn't have the chance to ambush us again," Kian said.

"I actually have an idea about that Kian," Kayla said. "Our uncle was always a man who liked his comfort, so he wouldn't be roughing it somewhere. And he would see it as beneath him to have his men stay with him, so we need to look for somewhere with multiple dwellings. Maybe a hotel? It's the off season for tourism, so he would have no problem finding rooms."

"There are some hunting cabins a ways north. He would be close enough, but all the way on the other side of the state park to stay hidden," Jase said. "That would also give him immediate access to nature for changes."

Walking back inside, his pants still undone, Lex said, "That sounds like the best alternative for him. They could easily break into a couple cabins and nobody would notice. My gut is saying they're closer though. They need to be able to hit us quick or escape like they just did. There are a handful of cabins within a few miles of here. I need to grab my laptop so I can check it out"

"I'm coming with you," Kayla said standing up and walking out the door behind Lex. He didn't seem surprised that she was following him. He didn't say anything on the drive to his house, but he did hold onto her hand, rubbing his thumb softly across her knuckles. They walked into his house and Lex headed straight for the office. Kayla stood in the living room remembering their first time together on that couch. She had changed so much since that night. All the fear that had been surging through her as she ran out to get away from Lex was gone.

The sound of him walking back out to her broke her out of her thoughts. "Everything alright

Kay?" Lex stood behind her and pulled her back snug against his chest.

"I was just remembering our first time, right here on your couch. It feels like so long ago. I wish I hadn't run from you Lex. I would change so much if I could go back." Kayla let his warmth ease some of the throbbing in her shoulder.

"It happened the way it was meant to babe. I ran from you ten years ago, and you ran from me. We both had to be ready, at the same time," Lex said quietly leaning down into her ear.

"All it took was getting shot," Kayla laughed.

"Yeah, maybe next time we need to get on the same page we can avoid bullets and bloodshed?" She could hear the smile in his voice.

"Sounds good to me," Kayla agreed.

Chapter 18

The next few hours ticked slowly by for Kayla. Lex was using his computer hacking skills to figure out the most likely hiding spot for Russell. Kole and Kian were out back to keep watch. Jase and Emma were in the front yard doing the same thing. Nobody in the pack trusted their former Alpha to not ambush them at any second. Kayla had tried to join them on lookout duty too, but that notion had been unanimously vetoed by her pack mates. After so much trauma physically, she didn't bother to fight it. Taking it easy would help her out later when she needed to fight. Food also helped her kind heal, and more was needed after the healing sapped all your energy. Needing some comfort food Kayla put a beef pot roast in a pan, settled some red potatoes, carrots, onions and garlic around the sides. Adding a little bit of water, and sprinkling seasonings on top she put it in the oven. The meat would help her body to recoup some strength, and everyone else needed to eat too.

Trying not to bother Lex, but wanting to be near him she walked into the living room and settled onto her lovely teal couch. Lex was on the opposite end, and when she stretched her legs out her toes brushed against his pants. Leaning her head back against the arm of the couch she relaxed and watched her mate work his magic. Kayla let her mind wander. It still felt a little strange to think of him as her mate, for so many years he was her oldest brother's best friend, and the man who had broken her heart. She tried to hate him for it for so long, and maybe she had even been subconsciously punishing him for hurting her all those years ago. No more running from her wolf, no more hiding her feelings, no more denying fate. Lex was her fated mate, and as soon as they could she was going to finish the claiming. Why bother cheating yourself out of whatever happiness you can find? Life really is too short for that.

After a few hours Lex said, "I can feel how happy you are right now," without even turning his head in her direction.

"Much in the same way I can feel how focused and determined you are. I don't want to distract you, I just needed to be close to you, I guess." Kayla hoped it was.

"You aren't distracting me; I like having you near. I am just sick of that monster playing games with the people that matter to me, and I want to find where he is hiding so we can flush him out. I need to do this. For my Aunt MaryBeth, your father, Emma, and every time your uncle looked at me like I wasn't good enough to be in his pack. But mostly for almost stealing my mate away from me before I even got to claim her."

"My uncle is what happens to a man who thinks he can do no wrong, someone who justified everything he does because he gets what he wants. He doesn't realize he has dug his own grave, his pride and ego will be his downfall," Kayla said quietly. "I should have waited for the rest of the pack. I shouldn't have run so far ahead to get to him. If they had all been waiting as wolves instead of in a truck, I wouldn't be here today. I got off lucky with that bullet. I won't be making that mistake again."

"You wanted to catch up to him, to make sure he paid for everything he has done. I get it, and any of us would have done the same thing. But you're right, we need to keep it together and be smart enough to stick together. Getting separated like that just can't happen again," Lex replied before going silently back to work on his computer again.

The oven timer sounded, beeping that her pot roast was finished cooking. Getting up, Kayla walked into the kitchen to check the dinner. Everything looked done, so she pulled it out and set it on the stovetop to rest a moment while she got plates down. Knowing that nobody was going to be able to relax sitting around the table Kayla brought two plates out back to her brothers. "Our uncle expects us to be soft, to let our guard down. Eat while you keep watch. You're going to need your strength," Kayla said as she handed the plates over. Both of her brothers took the food and were already digging in when she turned to go back inside.

Walking back into the kitchen she fixed two more plates up. Being a waitress for so long she was completely at ease with her arms loaded up like this. Stepping out on the front porch she handed one to Emma, and one to Jase. "I'll come collect the plates in a little while." Both offered her thanks as she headed back in.

Finally, she made up plates for herself and Lex. Bringing them out to the living room she set his on the coffee table in front of him, and sat down at his side. "You have to eat Lex. When you figure out where he is we all have to be in top form in order to bring him down."

Nodding his head at her Lex sat his computer on the table and picked his plate up. "I know. I'm so close, I can feel it."

"Then taking five minutes to shove some food in your face won't throw you off his trail," Kayla said bringing her fork to her mouth. "Besides, it's pretty good, if I do say so myself."

Lex ate without taking time to enjoy his food, but Kayla had expected no less. At least he was eating, that was the important part. There would hopefully be many more of her pot roasts in his future to appreciate more. She could feel her strength returning, the aches in her chest, and the throbbing in her shoulder decreasing with each bite she took. Food really was magic, and Kayla savored the effects of a good hearty meal.

When their food was all gone, she brought her and Lex's plates into the kitchen. Walking out back she picked up the plates Kole and Kian had stacked on a deck chair. Her brothers were out in the yard focused on the trees. The woods were filling with shadows big enough to hide in as the sun went down. Unloading the dirty plates in the sink she headed out front to get the rest. Emma and Jase were still on the porch, but they too kept their eyes on the trees surrounding the house. "Thanks Kayla, it was very good," Jase said politely. She brought them back into the kitchen. She rinsed off all the plates and stacked them in the dishwasher. Then she piled the leftovers into plastic containers for later, sure someone would eat them, before loading the pan into the dishwasher too.

Lex was talking excitedly to himself in the living room. Kayla got a sudden bad feeling that had her looking out the window above the sink. Staring for a few minutes she noticed very slow movement. There was a wolf scooting around on its belly towards the house. From this angle neither of her brothers would be able to see the intruder until it was right on them.

"Lex, there is a wolf outside heading slowly towards the house. Tell the others," she whispered knowing he would hear her.

Walking to the back door she opened it and asked Kian the first thing that popped into her head to get his attention without alerting the wolf sneaking up that they saw it. "Hey Kian, should I order us a pizza for dinner?" When he turned to look back at her, probably thinking she had lost her ever loving mind, she raised an eyebrow and motioned with her head in the direction she had seen the movement.

Understanding dawned on Kian's face a moment before a giant golden wolf ripped out of him, shredding his clothes in the process. As soon as his feet hit the ground, he was running in the direction Kayla had motioned. Kole took a moment longer to shift into a wolf, but he was following after his Alpha a heartbeat later. Lex, Emma, and Jase came through the back door then. "Should we change? It could be another trap," Emma said.

Before anyone could answer the sound of a fight echoed through the forest. Making up their minds everyone ran after their Alpha, their wolves clawing at their insides to get out. Lex was the first to shift, dropping down on all fours at the tree line. Then Kayla, and Jase, and finally Emma, as the newest wolf, she was still learning how to shift quickly. They all got to Kian just as he stood victorious over the light gray stranger wolf. Turning his head toward them, he had blood on his muzzle.

The other wolf was smaller than Kian, but most would be, and still larger than Kayla's wolf. He was bleeding from multiple bite marks all over his body, one of his front legs was bent the wrong way, and the paw was hanging limply. The pack gathered around him in a circle. Kian shifted back, and his raw power rippled across Kayla's fur in waves. Her brother was growing in dominance the longer he was Alpha.

"I will give you only one chance to explain who you are and why the hell you are in MY WOODS, before I end you," Kian yelled at the prone wolf at his feet. His eyes were blazing so brightly that it almost hurt to see them.

The gray wolf shuddered once and shifted back slowly, clearly in pain. The man's face drawn up in a grimace. "Caleb, name's Caleb. My Alpha loaned me out to Decker."

"Who is your Alpha?" Kian growled out between gritted teeth.

"Talon, from the Huron Pack," Caleb said, still laying prone, on the ground. Holding his shattered arm in the other.

"Why does the Huron Pack give a fuck about Russell Decker?" Kian asked. "I hear one lie and I stop listening," he said with menace.

"Decker promised Talon two strong women for breeding." Caleb was interrupted by a growl ripping out of Lex. Turning his head toward the big brown wolf Caleb said, "I swear it. My pack doesn't have mates, and the Alpha has decreed all the women as his to breed when he wants. He ordered my brother and I to bring the women back to him."

"You're coming back with me, you make one move and my pack will rip you to shreds, understand? Follow me." Kian waited until Caleb got to his feet and led him back to the house.

Kayla and Emma brought up the rear, Lex and Kole on either side of their prisoner. She knew that Kian wanted to get more information from him, and that they were targets sitting out in the woods. Kian walked straight into the house and pointed at the table. Caleb walked over and sat in a chair keeping his head respectfully down as the pack changed back from wolves.

"First, both of our women are already mated. Nobody will be taking them anywhere, ever. Second, how long before Russell and the others attack?" Kian asked.

"They don't know I am here. I came on my own. I am the best tracker in my pack, that's why my Alpha sent me. I followed your scent," Caleb said. "Decker plans on taking you out one by one, he is scared of a full-on fight with your pack. Talks to himself all the time about how he 'should have done Kian instead of Mick.' I knew when he shot at the cream wolf he wasn't going to be sending women back to my Alpha. Either he is going to kill me when he is done, or I go back empty handed and die then."

"So you figured on sneaking in here and getting the women yourself to take them back to Talon?" Kole asked.

"No, no, I've seen what happens to the women my Alpha beds. I was just curious about your pack, it's so different from mine. I wasn't going to attack, just watch you for a while, and then leave," Caleb said.

"Collecting intel to take back to Russell," Lex said shaking his head.

"No, leave the state for good. I was going to run. I know its cowardly, but the further away from the Huron Pack I got the more I never wanted to go back."

"What about your brother? You would just leave him?" Kian asked surprised.

"You misunderstand the ways of our pack. Gabe is my brother because the same man fathered us. We have two different mothers who raised us," Caleb said shaking his head. "He also fathered others when the mood struck. My paternity has done me no favors."

"Your father was Alpha wasn't he?" Kayla asked, understanding dawning. "That means that Talon is your brother too."

"He is the oldest of my father's children. But when my father was Alpha if a woman didn't want him in her bed that was her choice. Talon doesn't allow choice."

"Oh god! He is raping the women, Kian," Emma said with horror. "We have to help them."

"One problem at a time, love. Let's deal with my uncle, and then we can figure out how to help the Huron Pack," Kian said bringing Emma's hand up to his mouth for a kiss.

"You would help my pack?" Caleb said with shock.

"I'll let you live if you help us kill Russell, and then I will help you with your pack."

"Let me show you where he is hiding," Caleb said his eyes lighting up for the first time.

Chapter 19

Caleb wasn't telling them any lies, but for Lex that didn't mean that he could be trusted yet. Kian asked Kayla to warm him up the food they had for dinner in order to help speed up his healing. Lex watched the man's every micro-expression closely. Remembering that he had figured some things out just before Kayla spotted the intruder Lex said, "So while I was looking for where Russell was hiding I followed a hunch, and found a hidden back door access into your systems at Decker Construction. It looks like ol' Russell has been slowly trickling money out to fund himself. I can take it all back of course, but I wanted to talk to you about it first."

"He's embezzling company funds?" Kole asked. "I'm not surprised, it seems like the least fucked up thing he's done, but if you put it back won't it get the IRS all over our asses? The last thing the pack needs is the government's focused attention."

"Yeah, there is a definite possibility it will," Lex answered.

"I have an idea," Jase said speaking up from the other side of the room. "What if you used it to fund the pack? We could add to it over time, like dues, or taxes. Then we could vote on when and how to use it as needed." When everyone just stood there looking at him he went on. "I could handle that, kind of like treasurer or something. I like my money to make money, so it wouldn't be that hard for me."

"I don't see a problem with that, as long as everyone else agrees. I like the idea, and it seems like a smart move to modernize the pack a little," Kian said, his characteristic lopsided smile in place.

"I like the sound of that. Taking back what Russell stole, and making it work for the pack that he doesn't rule over anymore. Seems kind of robin hood-ish and fitting," Lex added.

"As long as we all get a say in how much the dues are, and what the money gets used for, I'm game," Kole said.

"This way we are all investing in the pack, and it makes it more ours," Emma nodded.

"Seems like a good idea. Jase, are you sure you aren't too smart to be on a construction crew?" Kayla added.

"Nah, I really like being on the crew. But I have always been fascinated with money, and the stock market, this will give me the opportunity to really make a positive impact on the pack," Jase beamed.

"That's settled then. Jase, you have constantly surprised me," Kian said giving him a slap on the back.

"We have a little bit of time while Caleb eats and heals, I can close the door, and reroute all of the money now. Just in case Russell has it rigged in case of his death or something," Lex said picking up his computer. "I wouldn't put anything past that man."

"Caleb, tell us more about yourself and your pack," Emma asked him as he ate Kayla's warmed up pot roast.

"What would you like to know?" he asked in between bites.

"For starters why you are so willing to help us?" Emma asked. "I believe you are, but honestly, I just don't understand your motivation. My pack, and all the people in it mean the world to me."

"The Big Woods pack is very different from the Huron pack. I guess if I had the kind of pack you do I would feel just like you do about it. My Alpha, Talon, has been killing off the men for a while. Slowly at first, so it didn't raise too much suspicion. Last year he claimed my sister's mate challenged him while they were out on a perimeter check. He killed him without any witnesses. That's just not how challenges are handled. Then Talon moved my sister and her small daughter into his house. He claimed it was to take care of them now that her mate is dead. But treats her as a servant, making her wait on his every whim. He won't let her move back into her own house."

"Because he can't use her to breed, he treats her like a slave?" Kayla asked.

"Yes, I think so. Gabe has always worshiped the ground Talon walked on, and he buys into everything our older brother says. He is the Second because he will wipe out anyone who looks at the Alpha the wrong way with an ever-increasing viciousness," Caleb said sadly.

"He likes all the killing for your Alpha, doesn't he?" Kian asked.

"Yeah, I'm afraid so. He won't be easy to take down, as he won't surrender, ever," Caleb said. "Russell is afraid of Gabe, and he watches him closely. He is anticipating a double cross, just not from me. If it weren't for my nose Talon would have ended me by now too."

"He uses you as a deterrent to keep the women he keeps from running, doesn't he?" Lex said from the other room. "Have you hunted any down and dragged them back to him kicking and screaming like his own personal blood hound?"

"No I haven't. Yet. But I think that's what he sees as my place in his pack, and its sick," Caleb said sadly. "I am not dominant enough to win a challenge against him."

"What about the other pack members? Are there any that could step in as Alpha once Talon is gone?" Kian asked.

"I just don't know," Caleb said sadly. Lex could tell it was the truth, but there was a lot missing they would have to deal with later.

"OK, finished. The money is back, with our own Mr. Jase Sanders as the executor of the pack's discretionary account. I will get you all the information later," Lex said shutting his computer down and setting it on the coffee table before walking back into the kitchen. He looked at Caleb. "How is the arm?"

"I can move the hand again. It's not one hundred percent, but it should hold my weight on all fours." He looked right at Lex as he answered.

"OK, here is how we do it. You take us there, and if you turn on any of us, your end will come slower than you would like, and there will be no help for your sister or the rest of the Huron pack from the Big Woods Pack. Got it?" Kian said.

"Got it," he replied.

Kian motioned for everyone to go out back, bringing up the lead. "Caleb is on point since he will be leading the way, with Kole and I on either side. I want Lex and Jase fanned out a bit, with Emma and Kayla in between. They should be sleeping, and the element of surprise will give us the advantage. We stick together, and nobody gets separated. We do this as a pack, or we won't all make it back here," Kian said and bending down in the darkness letting the golden wolf have his skin.

Caleb was the last to complete the shift, landing softly on the front injured paw, testing it out. As predicted, it held his weight. He looked back at the pack and headed off in the direction Kayla caught him coming from earlier.

Thinking to himself, Lex wasn't sure what to make of the man, but the possibility of finishing this tonight had a surge of adrenaline pumping through his system. Russell Decker had caused too much damage, played with everyone's lives too many times. His end would come tonight, one way or the other. Because Lex had figured out which set of hunting cabins Russell was hiding out in, and he would know if this Caleb steered his pack wrong. The sooner that evil bastard was rotting in a dozen pieces somewhere nobody would ever find, the sooner he could start his life with Kayla.

The moon was bright in the clear sky, glinting off the snow as they ran. The night cool and crisp. Somewhere off to the right Lex heard the sound of a rabbit scurrying off to hide as the pack thundered past. It struck Lex as strange that on a night they chased death he would notice just how beautiful their corner of the world was. Michigan winters could be brutal, but when the snow blanketed the ground there was a calm hush that settled over the forest. Glancing over at his mate running with complete focus Lex knew that if anything happened to her tonight there was nothing that would be able to hold the pieces of him together. He had to have faith in his Alpha and the strength of their pack.

The run took them thirty minutes following Caleb's cautious lead. They could have gone faster, but with an injured paw Caleb wasn't exactly ripping up the ground at breakneck pace. He never led them astray, much to Lex's surprise though. Maybe that guy was alright after all.

The pack paused about twenty yards away, and the two cabins were clearly visible through the trees. There was a small lake a few yards behind the cabins making an approach from there impossible. The pack waited while Kian darted back and forth between the trees getting a closer look. When he looked back at them and swished his tail the pack fanned out and closed in on the two cabins. Expecting that his uncle would try to take off running Kian slowly crept around the cabin his smell was coming from and waited at the back door. Kole let off a deep growl in the front. Inside the cabin they could hear Russell startle awake, not one to make rash decisions he was trying to figure out which direction the sound had come from.

Following the Alpha's lead to distract and confuse. Lex crept up to the second cabin, the one Caleb's brother Gabe snored loudly inside of. Lex let off a menacing growl of his own. The man inside wasn't pausing to listen and figure out the best escape route like Russell had, he jumped straight out of bed and Lex could hear him shifting, bones popping and reshaping, ready to fight. Just as the front window broke outward in a flurry of shattered glass was the softer sound of the back door to Russell's cabin opening. Lex hoped Kian had it handled. Because just then a gray wolf, only a shade deeper in color than Caleb's, but larger landed on all fours in front of him demanding all of his attention. Teeth snarling and snapping. This was a shifter who loved the fight, thrived on the violence of it. He would be all fury and instinct when he fought. Lex had to be smarter than his foe, that was the key to winning this.

Lex growled and pawed once at the ground inviting the other wolf to come for him. Force him to make the first move. Gabe leaped, and Lex dove under him snatching his back paw as the wolf sailed over him. Shaking that paw viciously in his jaws he heard the bones crunching. Kayla jumped in to help as Gabe pulled his foot away and spun ripping into Lex's ear. He felt the blood trickling down his fur. Kayla was on the gray's back, her teeth locked onto his shoulder ripping into him. Caleb came out of nowhere and before Lex could get to the other wolf's neck, Caleb's teeth clamped down until red splattered across the snowy ground. Gabe wasn't one to give in, staggering to fight all three of them off. It was no use though, and soon enough the big wolf lay on the ground, the life gone from his eyes. Caleb lifted his head in a mournful howl for his fallen brother. Lex and Kayla didn't stay to join him though, darting out back to help the rest of the pack dispatch Russell.

Jase was on the ground not moving when they got around to the other side of the cabin. Kole and

Kian were facing off with their uncle. Emma was standing guard over Jase. Kayla gave a yipping bark and raced between her brother's big wolves, her teeth finding Russell's side. Lex leaped into the fray. The four of them tore into Russell with abandon, ripping every time their teeth clamped down. Russell howled in pain, exposing his neck, and Kian bit into the softness there so hard when he shook his teeth his uncle was flopping limply like a rag doll.

Kian raised his head and howled his vengeance towards the moon. The Big Woods pack all lifted their heads and sang with their Alpha in joyous victory. The one who had caused them all the pain and suffering was no more.

Chapter 20

The pack worked together in the darkest hours before dawn to scatter pieces of the fallen wolves deeper into the forest, a good distance away from the cabins. Scavengers would take care of the rest, nature found a use for everything, even death. Anyone who had the misfortune to come across the bones would see only canine remains, which wouldn't raise any suspicions in this area. Kayla and Lex worked to gather up everything from Russell's cabin. They would sort through it all back home later, when everyone's energy wasn't tapped out from the fight. Fresh eyes would be able to see things they would surely overlook in their exhaustion. Kian and Kole watched over Caleb as he got all of his and his brother's things from the other cabin, he had been staying there too after all. They couldn't forget that Caleb had come to their territory working with the enemy. Kian didn't want him far away because they couldn't afford to trust him yet. The pack had a surplus of vacant houses still, so Caleb would be staying in one of the empty properties, close enough for him to be kept under constant supervision.

Jase had gotten tossed into a tree trunk and knocked out during the fight. He wasn't passed out for very long, but nurse Emma wanted him to take it easy for a little bit, so they were sitting in the small clearing out in front of the cabins. The old model truck Russell was riding in when he shot Kayla belonged to Gabe. They loaded everything they cleared out of the cabins into the bed. Since it was a four-door crew cab six of them squished together inside. The nudity didn't bother anyone, even packed so close together. After facing the things they did together, modesty fell to the way side. Jase volunteered to ride in the back with all the stuff, arguing that the fresh air would help clear the fog from getting his head knocked around when Kole tried to switch places with him.

The drive took a little longer than running back as wolves would have, but the truck couldn't be left behind. You don't spend so much time cleaning up loose ends, and then leave a giant 'look at me' red flag like an abandoned vehicle sitting around for someone to stumble upon. "Seems like we are getting to be a little too good at body disposal," Kayla muttered as they all staggered together into the house she shared with Kole.

"Yeah, I guess that's a skill we won't be bragging up on our resumes," Kole laughed sardonically. "I'm going to bed for a few hours now that we've rid the world of evil like the underrated, but bad-ass superheroes we are," he said tiredly as he headed off toward his room.

"Come on Caleb, you're going to be staying in the house next door to my place. We can take the truck," Jase said.

"In a few hours I want you to go with him into the Secretary of State, Jase. He can switch the title over, claiming his brother sold him the truck," Kian said. Both men nodded and headed out the door.

"Should he be allowed to go to sleep after hitting his head so hard?" Emma wondered.

"I think it'll be fine. Never heard of a shifter dying from a concussion, so I guess there's that," Kian said. "It seems a little anticlimactic, doesn't it? Russell's black cloud has been hanging over our head for what seems like forever, but I guess it's really only been two months. Come on Em, you look like you're about to fall over on your feet, let's go home."

When it was just the two of them left standing in the living room Lex turned to Kayla with a sexily shy smile in his warm brown eyes. "My place?"

Thinking that she didn't want to finish the claiming with her brother in the next room Kayla smiled at Lex and nodded. "Just let me grab some clothes for later." Running up the stairs Kayla grabbed the first things that her hands touched and tossed them into her largest sparkly tote bag. It was as she turned to head back downstairs that she realized she still hadn't put any clothes on. Running around naked immediately after a shift was no big deal, but this seemed like pushing that a little too far. She came up here for clothes, she should at least put some on. Pulling on some leggings and a long sleeve tunic she shoved her feet into comfortable sneakers, thankfully ones without laces. Grabbing her purse, she headed down. Lex had a pair of jeans on that bagged a little at the ankles suggesting they belonged to someone a little taller, when she walked up to him, but nothing else. "Stole those from Kole didn't you?"

"As an officer of the law I prefer the term borrowed actually." He took the bag from her and wrapped his other arm around her and they walked out into the early morning light together.

On the short ride to his house Kayla watched Lex, focused on committing every detail to memory. The way his wavy brown hair was just getting long enough to flop. The nose that had been straight before getting broken many years ago. The scruff along his jawline he would have to shave off for his work soon. But her favorite feature had always been his eyes. Those beautiful brown eyes of his. Her heart skipped a beat deep inside her chest at the realization that nobody would ever look into those eyes as they melted and churned to silver but her.

Lex turned the car off and turned to her with a smile. Her stomach filled with nervous excitement that felt like a thousand butterflies.

"No pressure Kay, but after nearly losing you, and wasting so long, I don't want to wait a minute longer to claim you as my mate." His voice cracked with emotion. "I can't live without you."

"Well then come on Deputy Kolter, take me on inside," she said, her blood already spiking with desire.

Not wasting time with a response Lex got out of the truck, and walked around to the passenger side. Opening the door, he scooped Kayla out and carried her all the way into the house like she weighed nothing. He didn't stop walking until they were inside of his bathroom. Leaning down Lex kissed Kayla like she was the only woman in the world, and for him she always would be. He poured all of the hungry desperation he felt into the kiss. Kayla got caught up in the turbulent storm raging between them and gasped and reached up into his hair holding him to her, letting his needs whip hers into a frenzy.

Pulling away from her lips Lex looked down at her, Kayla's blue eyes were already swirling with silver. The air filled with the scent of her arousal. "I planned on going slow, making it special, but I don't know that I can, Kay. Now that we are alone, I just, I almost lost you. I need you now, right now." Lex said setting her down on the counter, whipping her shirt up and off her.

"Yes, right now Lex, slow isn't our natural speed anyway. We crashed into each other; this should be just like that. Claiming is already special. We don't have to try." Kayla arched her neck inviting him to put his mouth exactly where she wanted it.

Lex kissed her neck, sucking, nibbling in a path down. He grazed his teeth across her collarbone, and Kayla's breath caught in anticipation, but he didn't break the skin. Instead, he licked a hot trail down to her breast, and she thanked everything that was holy in this world that she hadn't bothered with a bra. His tongue darted out against the pink peak of her nipple, before swirling around it, pulling it into his mouth. He sucked it hard, then wiggled his teeth back and forth on it, and Kayla let out a breathless moan. She wrapped her legs around his hips, her toes already curling.

Lex reached a hand down into her leggings. "So wet for me Kayla, if I have you every day of the rest of my life I will never stop being amazed at that." His finger slipped inside of her, and Kayla couldn't form a response. His mouth went back and forth giving both nipples equal attention, while his finger stroked deep inside of her. Completely lost to everything but the way Lex made her feel Kayla dug her nails into his scalp. Her breath already coming in needy little pants.

"Come on baby, you're so close," Lex said pushing a second finger deep inside of her. Kayla rocked desperately against his hand, the need building. Without slowing down Lex swiped his thumb across her clit and Kayla's body bowed back as she shattered. Her orgasm pulsing greedily around his hand.

Leaning back to look into her eyes Lex said, "I love you Kayla. I always have."

Throwing her arms around his shoulders and pressing up against him she replied, "Oh, Lex, I have always loved you too." He reached down between them with both hands, and Kayla heard her leggings rip as he pulled them away from her. He lifted her off the counter and turned her around as he stepped out of the borrowed jeans and kicked them away.

Kayla's hands rested on the counter, as she watched Lex behind her in the mirror. He ran his hands down her sides, and gripping her hips pulled her ass back toward him. Jaw clenched he looked up and locked eyes with her as he pushed inside and stilled. There was something so raw and intimate about watching their bodies join in the mirror. The almost feral look on his face, her flushed skin, both of their eyes molten silver. A tremble rippled across her skin, and unable to have him locked so still inside of her she pushed back against him. Lex let out a low growl. The sound vibrated his whole body. Moaning Kayla rocked back against him again. "So good Lex, it's always so good."

He ran his hand up her spine, and pushed her shoulder blades down slightly, understanding what he wanted she leaned down and tipped her ass further up. "Oh god," he said as the new angle had him filling her even deeper. Lex pulled out and pushed slowly back in again. His fingers digging into her hips. Kayla saw the exact moment his control snapped, and he pumped into her hard and fast, his speed building with each thrust.

"I claim you as my mate Lex, forever," she said gasping as she stared at the double crescent scars her teeth had made in his skin last time. She was almost there, another orgasm ready to rip through her body.

Lex leaned forward his hips not ceasing their gloriously punishing rhythm. He pressed a kiss against her shoulder, and with his lips still against her skin he whispered reverently, "I claim you Kayla as my mate. Forever won't be long enough." His teeth sunk into the skin as she cried out, her body clenching around his in its spasms. He looked up at her again, and just as her orgasm was waning she felt his dick grow impossibly bigger. She watched Lex's face as he came in jerking bursts inside of her, hijacking her own orgasm along for the ride.

Her body was still pulsing with aftershocks when her mate gave her the brightest smile in the mirror and reached back to turn on the water in the shower. He said, "Don't run, I'm nowhere near finished with you yet." Kayla was giggling as he pulled them both into the shower for round two.

Thank you so much for reading Lex and Kayla's story! I hope you loved them as much as I do.

Keep an eye out for the third installment in the Big Woods pack series coming soon!

~Cara~

About the Author

Hi, thanks for reading my book!

Hi, I'm Cara, which is my pen name, but I think of Cara as the most intimate and genuine part of who I am. I live in Michigan with my family, and our fabulously sassy dog. I drink far too much coffee, read all the books I can, hoard makeup, swear more than my mother would like, and dance around my kitchen -poorly- while I cook.

Find me on social media @CaraRomanAuthor! I have zero chill, and LOVE to connect with my readers. It's kind of the best thing ever.

Other Books By Cara Roman

Without A Wolf (Big Woods Pack Book One)

New in town, Emma Lowe was hiding a big secret. Wolf shifter Kian Decker needed to find out who she was, and why she was so very appealing to him. Turns out Emma wasn't the only one in town with secrets. Now their lives have been turned upside down, and they need to figure where they stand.

Still Yours

High school sweethearts, Ridge left Leigha shortly after graduation to follow his dreams of a career in the music business. Finding his success, but missing home, he is back twelve years later trying to earn a second chance with Leigha. Ridge isn't some eighteen-year-old teenager anymore, a lot has changed. Can Leigha open up and trust her heart to the man who broke it all those years ago?

Definitely Memorable

Caitlyn has always dreamed of vacationing in Ireland. After a disappointing divorce she decides its time she does something for herself. What she didn't count on was meeting a charming and devastatingly handsome Irishman, Nolan in a pub. Unable, or unwilling to deny the chemistry between them she throws caution to the wind embarking on a whirlwind romance. Love is never as simple as it seems though, and hers takes a course she never could have predicted.

Other Books From Baying Hound Media

Tell-Tale Hearts
by H.A. Blackwood

Darcy Ford is coming off an ill-advised relationship that ended in disaster. When she's at her lowest point, she meets a woman who takes her back ten years to a night of wild passion. A night when she met-and lost-someone who opened new worlds to her. A night where her heart was stolen. A night which was the beginning of this most recent disastrous affair. Only by re-telling these tales can she find her way back to her lost love and the return of her heart.